RUN

A **Vengeance** Novel

GREGG OLSEN

HOT
KEY
BOOKS

First published in Great Britain in 2014 by Hot Key Books
Northburgh House, 10 Northburgh Street, London EC1V 0AT

A CIP catalogue record for this book is available from the British Library.

ISBN: 978-1-4714-0185-5

1

This book is typeset in 10.5 Berling LT Std using Atomik ePublisher

Printed and bound by Clays Ltd, St Ives Plc

Hot Key Books supports the Forest Stewardship Council (FSC),
the leading international forest certification organisation, and is
committed to printing only on Greenpeace-approved FSC-certified paper.

www.hotkeybooks.com

Hot Key Books is part of the Bonnier Publishing Group
www.bonnierpublishing.com

For Adrian Greenwood

Chapter One

Cash: $17.00.
Dinner: My turn, spaghetti?
Days at this school: 155.
Texts from Caleb: 15 so far.
Plan: Find a way to tell him the truth.

MY NAME IS RYLEE AND I AM A LIAR, BECAUSE THAT'S WHAT I WAS RAISED TO BE.

I hear the water running in the bathroom sink and I know my mother will bitch at me for leaving it on. Even though I didn't. I just got home from school. Mom has been critical of me, while praising my little brother, Hayden—despite the fact he doesn't do much to deserve it. If he remembers to flush the toilet after a late-night pee, she practically does handstands the next morning. Mom has always been harder on me. She says that it's because I have so much potential. Which really means that whatever I've actually done so far has disappointed her.

Mom's been homeschooling Hayden since kindergarten. I could be homeschooled too, but I don't want to be. I want to fit in with other people. I don't want to be the loser at the mall who has no social skills, and doesn't know what's in and what isn't. How to wear my hair or whatever. You really can't learn all you need to know from TV or your Twitter feed, and contrary to what most people think: that all kids my age do is hang out online—it's not true for all of us. Not for me at least. I'm a watcher. I'm an observer. I like being out in the real world, mostly because my home life has always been so fake.

Not completely awful. Just totally fake.

I'm a sophomore at South Kitsap High School, in a rinky-dink town on Puget Sound, a ferry ride from Seattle. While I don't know for sure if I'm fifteen or sixteen—it's complicated—I do know that for the first time in a long time, I feel that I actually fit in somewhere. That's no small feat. We've moved fourteen times. I think. It's been so many times that I've lost track. But here in Port Orchard, no one asks any awkward questions about where we lived before because people come and go around here all the time. Across the inlet that fronts our town is the naval shipyard, a row of gray hulls in various states of disrepair. Moms and dads arrive in the naval ships or go out to the Pacific on their way to the nearest war. Kids come later and stay in crummy housing near the shipyard or the submarine base a little farther north. In a way, all the moving around that other people do makes me feel as if I actually am part of something stable.

Figure that one out and win a prize.

I hear Hayden squawking in another part of the house as I twist the knob to turn off the water. I look down at the toilet bowl, the water the color of sunshine, and I drop the lever and

8

the whirlpool sucks down my little brother's pee.

Gross.

I glance at myself in the large oval mirror hanging above the sink. I have never been what I'd call pretty. Not ugly either. Just average. Sometimes I wish that I had a big hairy mole on my chin or something that could distinguish me from the other girls who lurk in the halls at school with pleading eyes and awesomely heavy eyeliner that makes them look more glamorous than I am, at least at that particular moment. At my last school, I adopted a kind of Goth persona and really piled on the mascara. I'm talking about two extra coats of the blackest I could find. I catch myself smiling in the mirror, remembering. My dad—stepdad, really—thought I looked kind of slutty, but I told him that's what I needed to look like in order to blend in. My whole life has been about blending in, being invisible. And I just hate it. My hair is brown now—not chestnut, not auburn, just a nondescript brown, the color of the bark of the dead tree behind the house. I think my real hair color could be blond, but it has been dyed so many times I have forgotten what shade it really is.

"Rylee!" Hayden calls from somewhere in the house. The kitchen, I think. He probably wants me to fix him a chicken potpie or something as an afterschool snack. I keep telling him that he actually needs to go to school to have a real afterschool snack. I mean, look, he's here all day with a refrigerator and microwave at his disposal. He could have whatever he wants, when he wants it—the only undisputed benefit of being homeschooled.

I swipe a strand of my finally-past-my-shoulder brown hair

behind my right ear and imagine what I might look like if I had short hair again. Mom says that longer hair gives me more options, but the options that she provides only make me look like an unstyled country singer. But I'm not exactly Taylor Swift and, well, I can't sing anyway.

I turn toward the sound of my brother's irritating and agitated voice.

"Hurreeeeee! Ryleeeeee!"

Hayden seems louder and more urgent than normal, but it doesn't alarm me. He's always screaming about something. Screaming seems to be his way of ensuring that no matter what he says, it gets an immediate response.

I pull my hair from behind my ear.

"Coming, Hayden," I call as I leave the bathroom for the kitchen. The hall is dark and I flip the switch, but the lights don't go on. *Again.* The fuse has blown in this particular house practically on a weekly basis ever since we moved in. *House.* That's funny. That's the word that I always use. I don't think I've ever said the word "home" in reference to any place I've ever lived. I roll my eyes. I hate being the one forced to go into the dank, dark garage to get to the breaker box. There is always something in the way and it takes forever to get to that stupid box. I wish Hayden were more self-sufficient. But it's always down to me to get stuff fixed around here.

Hayden is on the other side of the kitchen next to the dinette set that Mom got from some guy on Craigslist two weeks ago. My dad was completely pissed off about it. He didn't think it was a good idea to answer an ad online and actually go to a stranger's house to make the purchase. But Mom dismissed it all.

10

"I don't want to live like a bottled insect," she had said.

I remember thinking of that disgusting tequila with the worm swirling around in the bottom of the bottle, but I was pretty sure Mom was speaking metaphorically, not literally.

"We have rules," Dad shot back. "And we have them for a reason." Dad is always like that—curt, direct, to the point. I have memories of when he wasn't quite so . . . so exact, so I know that somewhere behind his edicts and rules, he is a man who still knows how to smile.

Hayden is on the floor hunched over and when he looks up I notice two things. First, he's crying. That isn't unusual. Seems like he always cries whenever he doesn't get his way. I never get my way. The second thing I observe is so puzzling that it really doesn't compute. It's like my brain is stuck on a search engine to nowhere. I can't quite grasp it.

His white T-shirt is soaked in red.

Break a jar of raspberry jam? I think, though that possibility is so unlikely I can barely dismiss it from my mind before the grim reality of what is in front of my brother hits me. Hard. It is like a sledgehammer to the back of my skull. I lurch closer and Hayden looks up at me with the most frightened eyes I've ever seen.

He speaks in that scream-volume of his, though I'm inches from his mouth.

"Rylee! I think he's dead."

I throw myself down on the floor next to my brother and look at the blank eyes of my dad, staring into space. The room begins to turn as I try to grasp what has happened in our kitchen. Everything is spinning. I think for a second that this is what it must feel like to be really, really drunk. I push Hayden away and press my hands against Dad's face, then his neck. He is wearing a powder-blue shirt, gray trousers and a red tie. No, not a tie. It is a slash of blood that has emptied from the top of his chest, drained down his shirt, pooling on to the travertine floor—the floor that Mom had gushed about when we first moved into this house on Salmonberry Avenue. The black handle of a knife sticks out of his chest.

Dad *is* dead.

I don't cry. Hayden is crying enough for the both of us. I spin around. In my heart I knew that a day like this was always in the offing, that somehow darkness would come after my family. I knew that our life away from others, our life blending into the background of the world, could be undone by someone. Fear and the possibility that something like this was always there, has been what kept us together. It was also a barrier. It was what held us away from everyone that we ever pretended to know.

"Where's Mom?" I ask in almost a whisper.

Hayden has rolled his body into a ball, and is rocking back and forth like one of those weighted blow-up clown figures that give me the creeps. His light blond hair is compressed above his ears where his small hands clamp the side of his head as he tries to shut out everything. He's done that before. We all cope in ways that we can. Yet, as awful as this moment is, this isn't the time for shutting out the world. My heart is nearly heaving from my chest, but I do everything I can to offer him some reassurance. Despite the fact that our father is a bloody mess, we can survive. *If* we do the right things—and if we do them right away.

I lean closer and tug at his shoulder so that he will look up at me once more. *Listen to me.* "You have to get a grip on yourself, Hayden," I say, trying not to betray my real emotions. I continue to speak in a low whisper. I don't want anyone other than Hayden to hear.

My brother relaxes his hands, but doesn't remove them from his head. He looks at me. His blue eyes now look green with terror. He is small for his age, and he looks even smaller now. He's seven, but he could pass for five, though he never needed to. Age isn't crucial in homeschooling like it has been for me in public schools.

Hayden starts to speak, his words tumbling from trembling lips. He is nearly inaudible, but I catch each empty word. "Mom wasn't here," he whispers. "I was outside. I came in to use the bathroom and I heard something."

I grab his other shoulder and twist him around so that we are eye to eye. "What did you hear?"

I have his attention now. *Good.*

"Voices, Rylee," he says. "Yelling. A crash. Should we call 911?"

Hayden's eyes leave mine as they wander over our father and the knife that's planted like a stake in his chest. My brother is distracted by it and I need him to focus.

"Talk to me," I say, looking at him.

He doesn't say another word.

"Talk," I repeat.

Again nothing. His eyes are fixated on the blade.

I reach over and yank out the knife. It makes a kind of sound that I will never be able to fully describe. It is almost musical as it slides from our father's ribcage and out of the gash in his

13

chest. Not a pretty sound. But not all music is pretty. I know that from listening to my mother's CD collection on long car trips as we moved from place to place. I wipe the blade's handle with a kitchen towel that I retrieve from the counter. I don't want my fingerprints on the handle. I lay the knife gently on my father's chest. I don't know where else to put it.

"What happened?" I say out loud, to myself more than Hayden, this time no longer in a whisper. Whispering is getting me nowhere. I'm scared and frustrated and I know that talking loudly is foolish, but I somehow feel certain that whoever did this to our father is gone. Long gone.

Then it dawns on me. Our mother is gone too.

In that moment, in the space in which I want to tell off my brother, cry about my father, and search for my mother, I see it as my eyes follow the length of my father's shirt to the tip of his right index finger.

On that travertine that our mother went crazy over when we first moved in there were three letters written in blood. Dad's blood.

RUN

RUN is our family's code word. It tells me everything Hayden and I need to know. There's no calling paramedics; no 911 dispatcher to notify. There's no going through the house and pulling up family photos and squirreled-away scrapbooks. We never had those kinds of things anyway. Mom used to joke that if our house was burning down we'd have no reason to linger. We just didn't have anything worth saving.

14

"We're leaving now, Hayden," I say. I get up and he stays there, his eyes fixed on our father.

"What about Dad?" he asks.

I shake my head. In my heart I knew this day would come. Dad said it could. Mom promised that it would. "Nothing," I say. "We're going."

I reach into my father's jacket pocket and take his cell phone and wallet. He feels warm, but he is dead. I know that. His car keys are on the table. I take those too.

I yank Hayden to his feet.

"Now," I say. My tone surprises me. It is an order. Not a request. Not pretty please. An out-and-out demand. "We're leaving," I say with the same newfound intensity. "What part of getting out of here don't you understand?"

He wipes blood on his shirt.

I get behind him and shove him.

"I'm scared," he says.

"It'll be all right," I say, the first of many lies I will tell my brother in the days to come. I am in a strangely calm and frenzied state. Calm because in some peculiarly innate way I know what I must do, and yet my heart is racing and I'm frantically trying to coordinate my uncooperative brother and find my backpack by the door where I unceremoniously dumped it.

Before any of this happened. Before our world shifted to black.

"How come we're going out the back door?" Hayden asks, finally able to say something other than a whine about our predicament or tears for our dead father and our missing mother.

"We don't want anyone to see us. We'll cut through the woods, follow the creek to the road."

"And then what?"

I don't know the answer. I'm moving as fast as I can. Thinking as fast as I can. I grab a clean T-shirt from the pile on the table, an indication of what my mother might have been doing before our father's killer came into our house.

"Then we'll figure out the rest."

He looks at me with those dopey scared eyes. Thankfully, he doesn't say anything else as we bolt from our back door toward the ravine. Questions can only slow us down. And we need to get out of there fast.

Or we could end up with knives in our chests too.

Chapter Two

Cash: $88.00.
Food: None.
Shelter: None.
Weapons: None.
Plan: Don't have one.

A GRAY AND WHITE SEAGULL tussles with another smaller, nondescript shorebird over a French fry on the bench beside us. We are facing the Puget Sound Naval Shipyard in Bremerton. My money—if I had any to spare—would be on the scrappier little bird. Little birds can be formidable. Their fight is occupying Hayden's attention, which is good. The walk from our house was long and I'm tired. I've told my brother over and over that we are going to survive this and that we will find our mother.

"Where are we going to go?" he asks.

"I don't know," I say, immediately knowing that was the wrong answer. He looks up at me with eyes that tell me everything he's feeling.

Fear. Sadness. Shock.

I'm feeling all of those things too. I wonder if Hayden sees any of that in my eyes.

"We'll get through this," I say.

We need to pause. *Think.* We can deal with our grief later. I put my arm around Hayden's shoulder, feeling his bones underneath his dark blue hoodie and the clean T-shirt we exchanged for the bloody one I buried in the woods. He was always small for his age, but he feels like a toddler just now. I don't nuzzle him, because we're not the touchy-feely kind of brother and sister, but even so, I want him to know—to *feel*—my concern for him.

Even my love.

A big green and white Washington State ferry chugs through the choppy blue waters of Rich Passage to the dock in Bremerton. From our bench facing Sinclair Inlet, we sit in silence as the cars unload. I feel scared and empty inside, but I don't show it. I'm good that way. I once saw a girl get hit by a car and I didn't even yelp. I was ten then and my name was Jessica. I loved that name. I remember watching that green Honda Civic smack into that girl in jeans and a pretty pink top. I didn't even flinch. I didn't go to her. A lady standing next to me by the side of the street where it happened must have thought that my nonresponse was a result of shock, but it wasn't anything like that. When you have to pretend that you're someone or something that you're not you get pretty good at concealing emotions. Reactions, Dad says—used to say—are for amateurs.

"Maybe Dad wasn't really dead," Hayden says, the first of many stupid things that will pass from his lips as we sit there under a darkening sky.

Even though it might seem fake to him, I truly mean it when I pat him on the knee to offer some comfort.

"We'll be fine," I say, again nearly choking on the lie. I've counted the money in Dad's wallet. Yes, there are credit cards. But I know better than to use them. Credit cards can be traced. There is also a duplicate of Mom's latest driver's license—which seems weird, but I think I know why it's there.

An elderly woman with candy-corn orange and yellow hair approaches with a bag of stale bread and starts to feed the seabirds. The commotion seems to distract my brother and once again I'm grateful for the diversion. Ever since we left the woods behind our house on Salmonberry, he's offered up a mix of tears, sobs, and questions. None of which I really want to deal with.

I watch the woman and remember when Mom and I did that very thing, not far from here. I remember how the number of birds grew, one by one, until they encircled us. I remember how we worried they'd attack us like some old horror movie I'd seen and couldn't quite forget.

Hayden tugs at me and I'm snapped out of the memory. "Are we going to call the police so they can get Dad? We can't leave him there like he's garbage."

I am about to answer but then the woman smiles at us and I nod in her direction as though my little brother and I are just sitting watching the birds. I don't know why anyone would want to feed those nasty birds.

"We can't," I whisper loudly into my brother's ear. "You know the rules."

"We're alone," he says. "We can have new rules."

Hayden is young. Dumb. *Homeschooled*. He can't know what he's saying. I have to remember that in order for us to survive we have to remember my mother's number one rule: "Trust no one."

"We need to go to the drug store," I say, getting up and leading Hayden past the woman with the bag of stale bread. In a day or two, we might be eating that bread ourselves. Eighty-eight dollars won't last long.

"Can I get some gum?" he says.

I nod. "Sure. But only one package. We're on a budget."

Port Orchard isn't really such a bad town. The waterfront is pretty and the boats tucked into the marina make it resemble what I imagine New England might look like. That's one part of the country we've never visited or lived in. *Visited* seems like a better word. Our family never stayed anywhere very long. We walk past the library and I eye it as a place that we might be able to stay for the night, but I let it pass. It is small and the librarian there is one of those command-and-control types that lets nothing slip by her. She'd never close up for the night with two bookworm stowaways inside.

The drugstore clerk at Rite Aid watches me and my brother as we go inside. I'm going nowhere near the birth control section—the place where kids my age do most of their shoplifting. I'm heading toward the cosmetics section.

"You go pick out your gum and meet me at the counter," I say loudly to Hayden. I want the clerk to hear. I don't know why exactly, but when you feel you are being watched you almost want to give in to it instead of fighting it. I saw someone

20

on the news the other day say something about how she now assumes she's being filmed by some hidden camera and acts accordingly. She said something about how she's not paranoid, just resigned. That's kind of how I feel right now.

Hayden allows a tiny smile to cross his face. I wonder for a second if he's a good mimic or he really is happy to get that gum. Our dad was just gutted like a deer and Hayden's getting Bubble Yum as though nothing happened. At least, he's acting that way. The members of our family have always been pretty good at acting, so I guess I shouldn't be too surprised.

The cosmetic section is all pink and purple. I haven't put on much make-up at South Kitsap, my high school. I was going for a more natural look. Besides, I liked the idea of at least looking like myself, instead of a cartoon version of what a teenage girl would look like. I don't have any real close girlfriends to trade make-up tips. Sure, I can watch them on YouTube, but it isn't the same as being told what shade works best for you by someone who actually knows you.

I pick out a box of Nice 'n Easy hair dye, Summer Blonde. I feel the weight of it and compare it to other boxes. It seems the heaviest. That's good. It means there is more product inside. I've never had to do it myself, so I might need extra. I pick up another box, a darker color for Hayden. When reaching for a pair of scissors—I'll need those too—I notice blood droplets still on my hand. I don't care if I'm being watched on camera. I spit on my hand and rub the red off onto my jeans. *My jeans.* I realize right now that I have no other clothes. No underwear. Nothing. Everything I have is on my body now. I am an idiot. I should have grabbed more clothes for myself when I took that clean T-shirt for Hayden.

The scissors are twelve dollars and the two boxes of hair dye come to twenty-two dollars. That's thirty-four dollars. Add Hayden's treat and I've depleted my cash by nearly half.

I take the scissors and the hair dye to the counter and set them next to a box of hard-as-rocks Swedish Fish candy— *reduced for quick sale*. Right now it feels like I'm reduced for quick sale. I mean, I don't know how much time I have. Or if I'm even right about what happened to our father or where our mother is. I take a breath. Hayden's still deciding on gum. I know that he'll buy the sour green apple because he always does, but I say nothing to hurry him.

"Do you have any scissors on sale?" I ask the clerk.

She's a pretty woman about my mother's age. She has dark hair and the whitest skin that I've ever seen. Living in Washington, that's saying a lot. Her eyes are so blue I'm almost certain she's wearing colored contacts. I even tilt my head to see if I can get to see the edge of the lens against her iris for that telltale ring. They really are that blue.

"Over in crafts we have some that are on special," she says in a fluting voice. "Not as good as those Fiskars, but how much cutting do you have to do anyway? School project?"

"Yeah," I say. Another lie. I lie to everyone all the time. I have since I can remember.

"Here," the clerk chirps. Her name tag indicates she's called Christy. "Follow me."

We walk down the aisle past Hayden and I give him a little nudge. "We need to get going soon."

"Hard to decide."

Christy winks at Hayden. "The watermelon is our best seller," she says.

He nods.

"These are on special," she continues, pointing to some scissors, "practically a door-buster price."

"Practically," I say.

They aren't as nice as the Fiskars, that's for sure. But they are the right price—$4.95. I know I'll regret it later, but when you only have $88, you have to make the tough call.

Hayden meets me by the counter with his sour green apple gum and an Almond Joy candy bar.

"I got something for you," he says. His eyes meet mine and I see something in him that I haven't since I pulled that knife out of our father's chest. It's a kind of anxiousness. A kind of dependency, a neediness, to just go along with me. He's got no one else and he doesn't want to lose me.

Almond Joys are my favorite candy bar and he knows it. I don't think we can afford it, but our father is dead, our mother is missing, and I could use a little joy.

Even if it is only a candy bar.

We pay and head back toward the marina. The steady drumbeat in my head: *Dad murdered, Mom gone, killer gone*.

"Where are we going to sleep tonight?" Hayden asks.

The answer comes to me then and I point over at the ferry.

"On the boat, Hayden. That's where we're going to sleep."

My father left us the code word. I have his wallet, cellphone, and a little cash. Very little. I know better than to use the phone. I feel a little stupid that I thought of it just then. I fish the phone out of my backpack as Hayden and I make our

23

way to take a seat on the foot ferry from Port Orchard, across the inlet to Bremerton and the ferry landing. I look around to make sure no one is watching. I take out the cellphone battery just to be sure. I know about GPS and I know that if anyone is trying to find us, they will probably see if the phone pings any cell towers. On my dad's key ring is a small brass key. I know that the next morning will be our only chance to use it.

Hayden whimpers about something, but I don't listen to him. At least he isn't crying. I can't deal with tears right now. We have to figure out how we're going to survive and find our mother.

If the man we've been running from all our lives hasn't killed her.

I chose the ferry for our first night for no real good reason. Just because I saw it and it seemed like we could hide there. Also, because we're traveling eastbound to Seattle there is no ticket needed. Nothing to deplete our cash. We barely have enough money for the worst motel in Bremerton for one night. The *worst* motel. Again, that's saying a lot.

I close my eyes to shut out the undulating noise of the foot ferry's old motor, my brother's whining, and the two other passengers, who seem to be planning their date night in Seattle. I hope that if I live long enough to have a real boyfriend we don't have to be so stupid as to look at a newspaper for ideas on what to do on a date. I concentrate on what I saw at the house, our kitchen. Dad's dead eyes stare at me. He was on his back. A chair had been moved from the round table. A struggle? But not much of one. The knife was not one of ours. It was a hunting knife. We don't hunt. We're the hunted. Whoever came to our house threatened Dad. There were papers spread on the kitchen table. Why hadn't I taken a moment to see what they were? I answer my own question. Because I was scared. That's why. Mom's purse was on the counter. Why didn't I grab *that*?

And, really, why didn't *she* take it with her?

I THINK OF HER JUST THEN. She is sitting in the kitchen looking at something, some papers. She looks upset, but I breeze past her to get something from the refrigerator. I'm late for school and I don't want to miss the bus, no matter how lame taking it to school is. Dad is already gone for the day. Mom says my name, but I don't even turn to say goodbye. I just don't want to be late for that stupid bus.

Mom has blond hair. Her eyes are blue, the one constant in her appearance. Her name is Candace. A dumb name, I think. She goes by the nickname Candy. At the time we selected our new names, I didn't like what she'd picked. Candy seemed like the name of a trailer-park mom. My mother isn't trailer park. Not at all. She is strong and beautiful. She is pretty—no matter what color hair she has. I never looked like her, even when we wore Mommy and Me outfits. I don't hate her because she is beautiful. I only wish that I had more of her in me.

We had traditions that were unlike those of any of the other kids that I knew at school, my only window to what real people did. If I didn't go to school, I would have had a completely warped view on family life. Maybe everyone *was* like the Kardashians in one way or another and I just didn't know it? I could almost see the look on Dad's face when it was time to leave whenever we were on the run. His anxiety.

The way his eyes narrowed and sweat collected at his temples and he'd withdraw a little. I knew that he was worried that we'd be found. We called the nights we left a place to move on "the switch". We always had pizza while we did it. The person who ate the last slice got to hold the glass bowl with a bunch of names of towns that were written by Mom on small, fortune-cookie-sized pieces of paper.

"Why do we go to so much trouble?" I once asked.

Dad looked at me quizzically. "How do you mean?"

"We could just pick a town. We don't have to make a game of it."

"There's security in randomness," he said.

My mother nodded. I think her name was Caroline that time. She always took a C name.

"If we are thinking of a place, making plans for a place, then it can be found out. If we are random, no one can know where we're going, honey. You know, because even *we* don't know until we make the run."

It sort of made sense, in the way that parents sometimes can make the most ridiculous things seem normal. Like Santa Claus. Like the fact that only old people die. That all dogs go to heaven. Speaking with authority is something practiced over time. I need some of that strength right now. I have a little brother and a missing mother to worry about.

Dad's face comes to me just then. I remember the first time I saw it. He'd lived in the apartment next door. We'd never talked to anyone. Mom wouldn't. But he was always there in the hall, smiling. Waving. Being nice. I was too young to know that he was interested in Mom. I didn't know that when she let him inside her life she was taking a huge risk. Not the same kind of a risk that came with the man we'd been running from. But a risk of the heart. I think I loved him as much as she did. He was our lifeline to the outside world. Never judgemental at the craziness that Mom created out of a dark necessity.

THE FOOT FERRY'S ENGINE RUMBLES. A woman with glossy black hair and blusher laid down in stripes sits next to me and sets down her bag. It is one of those oversized quilted bags with the delicate print of nautical emblems forming a border—fishermen's knots, seahorses, life preservers. Nantucket, grandma-style. The bag is unzipped and its opening is like a gaping mouth of a bass with a fat wallet between its jaws. She's exaggerating her interest in a man, a few years older with a splash of silver on his sideburns, who's sitting next to her in the way that suggests they really don't know each other. At least not yet. I watch Nantucket carefully from the corner of my eye. I turn to Hayden and pretend to talk to him, but with the rumble of the boat, I don't need to use real words. I know what I'm about to do is wrong, but in the scheme of things of what I will come to do to survive, it is small. Tiny. A puff of air. I reach down and in one sweeping motion I take her wallet. Still pretending to talk to my little brother, I put the wallet between my legs and open it, fishing for the folded paper of money.

Success! I pull five bills from the wallet. I don't even look to see if they are larger than ones, though inside, I'm praying that they are. Nantucket looks over at me and my heart sinks like a deep-sea diver's weights. I'm in trouble. She must have seen me do it. I don't know what I'll say to wriggle out of it. My heart starts racing and I prepare my excuse, my professed sorrow. I'm on drugs. I'm a klepto. My brother made me do it. Not the true reason—that I need the money because my dad is dead and Mom is probably being held captive by some monster.

Her look, thankfully, is only a glance in my direction.

She turns to the man and I drop the wallet back into her purse. My brow is soaking and I try to shake off my anxiety. *I did it. I got the money*. The boat docks and Hayden and I are fifty-five dollars richer.

But our dad is still dead.

And Mom is missing.

I can't stop thinking of her and him. I can't let go of the images of what happened to him and what might be happening to her. I want to go somewhere and scream at the top of my lungs. Words that would indicate how unfair things are. How broken I feel. Words that could convey how my being born into this life was unjust, unwarranted. Mean. I want to be the girl who laughs. The girl who has a boyfriend. I want to be the girl who tells others that she hates her mother even though she doesn't. But I am none of those things. I don't think I ever will be. I am trapped by circumstances, but I vow that I will never be a victim.

I'll leave victim status to *him*.

Chapter Three

Cash: $114.05.
Food: Green apple bubble gum, Almond Joy.
Shelter: None.
Weapons: Crappy scissors.
Plan: Still thinking.

IT IS A LITTLE AFTER eight p.m. when we get on the Bremerton to Seattle run, a crossing that takes about an hour. The boat is the *Walla Walla*, a name that I think fits the circumstances of my life right now. Walla Walla is also the city where the state's toughest prison is located. Hayden always thought the name was funny, but he's not laughing now. Neither am I. After making a stop in the women's bathroom, I give Hayden some quarters for a Kit Kat from one of the vending machines. I don't care that he hasn't eaten a decent meal since lunch. I have other things to think about. The ferry will cross back to Bremerton and then back to Seattle, then back to Bremerton, with a final return to Seattle well past midnight. I study the routine of the ferry's crew. I know they won't kick us off, because we're behaving. We take a seat next to a sepia-toned photograph of Princess Angeline, Chief Seattle's daughter: born in 1820, died in 1896. She has skin weathered like silver driftwood and her eyes are wide and light in color—like amber beach glass, I think. She's watching me as I plot my way to the end of the night. I know some people believe that her spirit still walks the Seattle waterfront, her ancestral home taken over by white settlers more than a hundred and fifty years ago. Those who see her wandering the streets closest to Elliott Bay insist that she always smiles knowingly at them, then shakes her head and disappears into thin air. I don't know if I believe any of that, but I have no doubt that if she were on the ferry, I'd ask her how she does it.

I want nothing more than to disappear right now.

My brother and I are seated in a booth near the bathrooms. These are farther away from the snack bar and don't get as much foot traffic as those next to the areas where the majority of ferry passengers congregate. I watch a crewman go into the men's room with a bucket in one hand and cleaning supplies in the other. I know that inside the door is a sheet of paper that indicates when the restroom was last cleaned.

"Say something, Rylee," Hayden says. Chocolate marks his upper lip, but I say nothing about it. I don't point. I don't kid him for looking like a pig.

"Sorry," I say. "Just thinking. Give me a minute." My eyes leave Hayden's chocolate-lip and zero in on the crewman with the bucket as he departs the men's room for the women's. We sit there as the cars offload. The bang-bang of their tires as they hit the ramp is almost like a drumbeat. Mocking. Telling me that I had better get things in motion. Reminding me that time is passing. Somewhere out there, our mother is being held captive. She always said this could happen. I don't know what is being done to her for sure and I want to throw up, but my stomach is empty.

When we are halfway to Seattle, I say to Hayden, "I need you to do something for me."

He looks up. "What?"

"When I tell you, you'll need to plug the toilet with a big wad of toilet paper."

He seems confused, but says nothing.

"Once the water gets flowing, you'll need to hide."

He thinks I'm a moron, but I don't care. I have a plan.

"Where?" he finally asks.

I tilt my head in the direction of the restroom. "There's a storage cabinet in there. They use it for paper towels and stuff. The lock is broken."

"How do you know that? And where will I hide?"

I let out a muffled sigh. More of a sisterly reaction than how I really feel right now. But the truth is Hayden doesn't get anything. And I'm tired of his constant questioning. If he wanted to be in charge of everything, then he should have been born first.

"I broke it, that's how I know," I say, reeling in my annoyance. "And you'll hide in there."

Once more the look. "How could you have broken it? You've never been in *that* bathroom."

"You're not going into the men's room," I say, softly, trying to control my exasperation. "You're going in the women's room."

"But, I'm a b—" he begins to protest.

31

I put my fingers to my lips, signaling my little brother to hush. I want to say the words "Shut up, you brat!" but that won't do. This is about being able to disappear, like Princess Angeline.

"It will work," I say. "Trust me. No one will know a damn thing."

He looks startled by my language, the least of my worries. And, really, not that bad, if you ask me. I know plenty of worse swear words.

"After you hide, I'm going to get help. A man will come in there and shut down the toilet's water flow. Since it's the last run of the night, he'll leave the mess for the morning crew to clean up."

"How do you know that?" Hayden asks.

"I know it from watching him. He's never in there long enough to do the supposed cleaning of the bathroom. He's a slacker. Big time. Just goes in there for fifteen seconds to check off the fact that he was in there by putting his initials on the sheet posted next to the door."

The bathrooms on the ferry are old-school, smelly and noisy. The women's room is bad enough that I don't even want to imagine what shape the men's room might be in. Having a little brother who never manages to leave the bathroom in any semblance of cleanliness gives me a pretty good idea. Add a hundred men and boys on a ferry run with the complication of the motion of a ferry boat and it isn't hard to imagine. No one likes to sit on a wet toilet seat, right?

I watch the security guard in his cheap black slacks and dingy white shirt that has been ironed only in the front. He looks nothing like someone who could help me. Even so if I were any other girl in the world, I'd fling myself in his arms, crying about my father, begging for the security guy to help me find my mother. But I'm not any girl. I'm a girl who knows that no one can be trusted. Especially anyone working in security, or the police. I know that many of them mean well, but they have too many rules. And when they had a chance to help my family, they failed. I will never trust them. I see how the police have done things to help others. My family, however, wasn't one of those others. Not by a long shot.

I AM PLAYING BACK EVERY moment after the bus stopped on the corner and I walked toward our house on Salmonberry to find Dad lying in a pool of blood on the floor. Caradee and Gemma got off the bus with me, and they stopped to catch a quick smoke before ducking into their houses. Caradee is a sullen girl who hides behind a frown. Her nose is in a permanent state of being scrunched up, like she just smelled something in the refrigerator that went bad. Or maybe it's the halo of cigarette smoke around herself that she's smelling. She stinks like an old smoky motel room or maybe even a wet ashtray. Gemma is the more pleasant of the two. She has nice, blue eyes and zitless skin that suggest either good hygiene or an acne prescription from a dermatologist. She always smiles at me and occasionally asks me over to her house at the end of the street, but I almost always come up with an excuse to get out of it. I have no room for girlfriends in my life. I do the bare minimum to be friendly without getting close.

Gemma and Caradee talk incessantly, which suits me. Their chatter can fill the air. It means that all I have to do is nod and say "Oh my God" or "No way!" or if it's about a guy, "What a prick." As long as I punctuate their silliness with some kind of supportive remark they think I like them. Having them think that is fine. I don't want or need any more enemies.

I left the girls smoking on the corner. It's not that I felt some kind of urgency to get home. You know, like I *knew* something was wrong. I'm not that dramatic. You don't have to be dramatic if you've lived my life, anyway. Drama has just always been there. No need to create it.

AS I SIT HERE NOW on the *Walla Walla*, looking out at the city of Seattle as it blushes pink with the sunset over the Olympics to the west, I think about what I might have seen or heard. What might be helpful later. Hayden has taken one of every brochure off the rack by the bathroom—destinations for tourists, real-estate offerings for locals. Right now he's looking at a brochure for whale watching on Neah Bay, over on the Olympic Peninsula. He seems occupied. It gives me a break, time to replay more of what happened.

Colby, a neighbor's cocker spaniel with sad droopy eyes, barked at me as I passed by—after I left Caradee and Gemma. Even though that dog knows me, and even though I gave him treats nearly every day all school year, he still treats me like I'm a stranger on my own turf, and it unnerves me. Dogs, I know, can be very smart. As I rounded the corner of our street, I stopped a moment to shift my backpack from one shoulder to the other. And then I noticed the fire department truck flashing its red strobe over the soggy green grass of the white house with black trim next door. My heart beat a little faster.

34

I hoped that Mrs. Swanston was all right. She and her husband have been so nice to me and Hayden. Not grandparent-nice, but as close as we could get to that kind of relationship. The aid car had been there three nights ago, and once the month before. The lights were flashing as I approached, and my eyes widened . . .

"She's going to be okay," a young paramedic told me when he saw the look on my face. He was handsome. Fireman-calendar handsome, I thought then. Even for Port Orchard. He knew how I felt, because in that moment I wasn't wearing the mask that is my second nature.

"That's good," I said.

Peter Swanston came over to me. He is in his sixties, maybe even a bit older. His eyes were rimmed with red. He breathed in short puffs of emotion.

"Rylee," he said in that sandpaper voice of his, "Steffi is going to live to make trouble another day. It's just her diabetes. We have to get that in check."

I wanted to hug him, but I didn't. I have never really hugged anyone but my mom, dad and brother. Instead, I nodded silently and, for the first time, I noticed Dad's car in the driveway. With everything going on around me, it didn't register as odd that his car was there, that when I went inside a minute or so later that he'd be there. It was too early in the day for Dad to be home.

"Steffi had a fit that the sirens were so loud," Peter was saying. "She thought it would blast people out of the neighborhood. You know, she doesn't like a show of things."

"Tell her I'll be over tomorrow," I said, not knowing then that it was a commitment I wouldn't be able to keep.

"Your company left. Like a bat out of hell," Mr. Swanston said by way of answer. I said nothing, still shaken about the aid car and Mrs. Swanston's condition. I wasn't thinking of any company that came and went. Just the thought of that nice old lady and her umpteenth medical emergency.

Then I went into the house, dropped my backpack by the door and went to turn off the running water in the bathroom. And after that, my brother and father in the kitchen. Red everywhere.

THE FERRY LURCHES TO A STOP and I'm sitting here thinking, remembering, registering Mr. Swanston's remark properly. Mr. Swanston had seen a visitor, a visitor who had left in a hurry . . . when the sirens came screaming down our street. Maybe my father's killer, my mother's abductor, had been scared away by the sound? Maybe he thought the police were closing in on him.

A couple who smell like a cloud of body spray and marijuana scurry past, toward the stairway that leads to the car deck. A woman in a black suit with a carnation-pink scarf follows. Hayden, still looking at the breaching killer whales on a brochure, is motionless. I don't move.

I wonder if Mom told the man who killed Dad that she'd already called the police. It was something she taught me at a very young age.

"Even when your back's against the wall, you lie," she told me when I was eight or nine. "You tell him that you've pushed a panic button or something and the police are minutes away."

Him. I'll come back to *him* later.

I turn to Hayden and nudge him away from the real-estate magazines that hold his rapt attention.

"Let's move now."

He nods slowly. "Okay. I'll plug the toilet."

NOT SURPRISINGLY HAYDEN DOESN'T LIKE the idea of us taking over the women's restroom but I figure it will be a safer location than any other to stay the night. At one time there was a black vinyl couch in there, a place where nursing moms are invited to sit and rest with their babies. But when I go in there to break the cabinet lock I notice the couch is gone that night. Or maybe it was on another boat? Hayden and I wad toilet paper in the first toilet and send the water overflowing. I lead him to the back of the restroom and the storage locker. I push some rolls of toilet paper aside and he goes inside. He's compliant and I wonder why he doesn't protest at least a little. I don't want him to, of course. But still? I shut the metal door and it seals like a rickety coffin.

"You're not locking me in, are you?" he says, muffled behind the door.

"No. And be quiet."

I hurry out to find the lazy ferry worker. He's chatting up a woman too young and too smart for him, I think.

"Excuse me," I say, "but someone clogged the toilet in the bathroom."

He looks at me with irritated eyes.

"Jeesh!" he says.

"It wasn't me," I shoot back. No one wants to be the source of a toilet clog. "It was like that when I went in there."

"Just a sec," he tells the woman. She looks relieved when he walks toward the bathroom.

"He'll be right back," I say.

She mouths, *I hope not.*

I smile.

The lazy/horny crewman does exactly what I thought he would do. He stops the flow of water and puts an out-of-order sign on the door, locking it. I hover by the brochure rack until he goes off looking for the woman he was chatting up—smartly, she has left for her car. When it is safe to do so, Hayden opens the door and I go inside and turn the lock. We are safe. We are alone. We're also in a bathroom, which isn't anything to brag about. But what choice do we have? We don't have any place to go. We don't have any family. We are alone.

I look at Hayden. "We'll be fine. Just fine."

He doesn't respond. Being shut in a storage locker has made him mute. Like I said, I wonder how much his life so far has affected him that he has this instinctive response to these situations? But the fact is I don't need him peppering me with questions and complaints. Even worse, I don't need him crying. Because if he cries again, then I will fall apart too. I'm not without feelings. I just do my best to hold them inside because that's the only way anyone can get through the really hard stuff. My mother told me that.

I remove paper towels by the fistful from the dispenser next to the sink and lay them on the floor. I'm not trying to make a bed, not in the true sense. I'm thinking like a hamster or gerbil and just trying to get some insulation between me, Hayden, and the hard, cold tile floor that will surely suck any of the warmth our bodies can generate in the short night in the bathroom. With the engines turned off, the boat becomes surreal in its silence. I never knew a quiet as loud as the roaring of the engines. Hayden snuggles next to me and I cradle him like a baby.

"I'm scared, Rylee," he finally says.

"We'll be fine," I say for the umpteenth time.

"I know," he says, in a way that almost suggests that he really does have faith in me.

I put my fingers to my lips and Hayden closes his eyes. I wait. Keeping your emotions inside is a bit like holding your breath. You can only do it so long or you will pass out. Or worse, if you don't suck in any air, you will die. I feel his breathing slow. I feel the weight of his body increase as he falls into much-needed sleep. Then, and only then, one tear manages to crawl out from the corner of my eye and I just let it roll, then another. My face is hot and wet, but I do not move my body. I do not wake my brother in the middle of my moment of weakness. Mom told me that she learned to control her feelings. She said that she knew that emotions only made the punishment greater. Her reactions, she said, made the man who held her captive, who hunted her, dig into her misery and revel in it. Don't get me wrong, Hayden isn't like that monster. Not at all. He is good. He is my brother. He needs me to be strong because I'm all that he's got.

Hayden is asleep and I gently lift him away, deeper into the nest of paper towels. I get up and look in the mirror. My hair is the longest it's been in years. I realize I love it even in its current nondescript brown. I can twist it into a luxurious ponytail. I can French-braid it. I know that I should not even be thinking about my hair, but suddenly I feel really attached to it. My mother is missing. My father is dead. My brother and I are alone. I turn in the dim light of the ferry bathroom and hold up my hair with one hand. I reach for the crappy scissors and start cutting. Locks fall like autumn leaves over the dingy countertop and into the bottom of the pitted white sink. I cut and I cut. Tears roll down my cheeks but I don't make a sound. I have lived a life in which I've had nothing of my own. No family pets. No birthday parties with relatives. No true friends. Nothing to brag about. Nothing to tell the world that I am here, that I am an individual. Now even my hair must go. I cannot look like the girl that lived on Salmonberry. Hayden is a little boy. Little boys blend in. A girl never does. A girl's hair, even in its nondescript brown, can be memorable.

"She sucked a strand of her hair, ugh!"

"She had soft, loopy curls."

"Her cut was terrible."

"Her bangs swallowed her eyes."

I can no longer look like the me of Salmonberry Avenue, the me of South Kitsap High School. Even though I'm not pretty like Mom, I am young. A girl. Mom always said that a teenage girl is remembered by other girls, other boys, all men. I guess this is flattering but it's also creepy.

Mothers look at girls too, and they see a younger version of themselves.

I open a box of dye and apply it with the thin plastic gloves that come in the box. I smell the chemicals as my hair eclipses from brown to blond. I rinse in the sink, the acrid odor wafting

40

through the still air of the bathroom. I use the paper towels to wring out the water and then, in what I think is a brilliant move, I turn on the hand dryer and rotate my head against the warm spray of air. I am in Maui. I am in Tahiti. I'm on the beach and I have a tan. A handsome boy looks at me and I smile.

The dryer stops and I look in the mirror and I see her. *Mom*. I look just like my mother. It was unintended genius.

Hayden, awakened, seems to agree.

"I miss Mom. Do you think they found Dad?"

I indicate the second box of hair dye. "Your turn, Hayden."

My brother knows what to do. He climbs up on the counter and lays his head in the sink as I wet his hair with lukewarm water. It reminds me of when he was a baby and Mom washed him in the sink instead of the tub. I hold onto that memory for a second. He scrunches his eyes shut as I rub in the dye. When I'm done, he will be transformed. He'll no longer be the little boy with the shock of blond hair, the one that makes him look like he's stepped out of the home page of a cute kids' clothing website. While he was getting his disgusting green apple gum, I was shopping for a dramatic change, a way to erase what happened to us. To no longer be the kids we were. I didn't really notice the name on the dye box until that very moment.

Dark and Dangerous.

I break into a smile for the first time in hours. It is a weak smile and kind of twisted, but it's real. It makes me think of my mother—she would have laughed at my choice for Hayden's dye job. And I would have laughed right along with her.

Chapter Four

Cash: $113.30.
Food: None.
Shelter: Ferry bathroom.
Weapons: Same crappy scissors.
Plan: Going to the bank.

THE NEXT MORNING WE SNEAK out of the bathroom. The front page of *The Seattle Times* stares out from the blue metal vending box and my heartbeat starts hammering like a nail gun. Fast. Despite a mostly sleepless night, I am now as awake as if I'd guzzled ten lattes in a row. The ferry smells of fresh coffee and donuts, but as hungry as I thought I was, I no longer want to eat. I cannot focus on anything—only the photographs of our house in Port Orchard and the image taken of me at the beginning of the school year.

I despised that photo back then.

I hate it even more now.

My eyes follow the headline.

PORT ORCHARD MURDER MYSTERY STUNS NEIGHBORHOOD

Hayden studies the newspaper's front page with the same intensity as I do. Glancing at him I see that his mouth is open and I'm pretty sure his expression is a genuine jaw-dropping gawk. I pull three quarters from my pocket, damp from a night in the bathroom, and slot them into the machine. The coins fall one by one. I remove all the copies of the day's edition and, with a quick glance around me, I shove all but two in the recycling box. I hold out one for Hayden. One for me. I don't want him hovering over me. I need to see what the reporter scraped together in the hours after our father was murdered.

We slide into a hard, molded plastic booth near the galley, across the boat from Princess Angeline's portrait. Her beer-bottle glass eyes still penetrate mine when I look over at her, but I don't care.

My heart is pounding and wetness blooms under my arms and wicks into the only shirt I have. But right now I feel more anxious than gross.

The victim was Rolland Cassidy, 42. Missing are his wife, Candace, their daughter, Rylee Ann, 15, and their son, Hayden Joseph, 7 . . .

No one ever calls us Rylee Ann and Hayden Joseph, and since neither of us had those names a very long time, they don't incite much recognition. My photo with my old hair does, however. The picture of the house does.

The last family member seen was the 15-year-old girl, who talked to a neighbor around 4 p.m.

"Things like this don't happen here," said the neighbor, who preferred not to be identified. "Things like this don't happen to nice people like the Cassidy family either."

I want to call Mr. Swanston, because I'm pretty sure he's the unidentified neighbor, and tell him how this is exactly what happens to nice people like us. Did he think that evil only comes after the bad? That darkness only seeps into a corner?

Hayden looks up at me from the paper. He reads at a third-grade level, something that Mom said could only occur because of homeschooling. It was the only thing—besides the always-available refrigerator—that was good about homeschooling. His eyes are pooling with tears.

"Are we going to find Mom today?" he asks.

I put my arm around him. I cannot answer that question and if I did and I told the truth, he would shatter right there in that Formica booth. I can't have that.

"Look, don't cry. Don't make a move. I'm getting you a hot chocolate."

"I don't want any."

"I don't care," I say as I start to get up.

"Is everything all right?" A woman in a maroon sweater and expensive jeans says to me.

I look at her. "He's fine. He wants a hot chocolate and I don't think it's a good idea. Sugar, makes him hyper."

Her face is kind and she nods. "My boys lived on sugar and they turned out all right. One's a doctor."

I smile politely and shrug my shoulders. I don't know why she had to add that her son's a doctor. I imagine she probably worms that detail into any conversation she's in. I get that she's proud of her son, but honestly, why bring *that* up?

I turn to Hayden. "Stay right here. I'll get you that hot chocolate." I look over at the woman. "And a donut too."

As I loop around the ferry with the speed of an Olympian, I notice a man looking at the *Times* front page. Me and that bad school photograph again. I drop three quarters in the vending box on the opposite side of the ferry and take out the rest of the papers. I dump them in another recycle box. Even though my hair is way shorter and blond now, I'm not taking any chances.

A few minutes later I return with the hot chocolate, a coffee and two maple bars. I don't need the energy, but I do need something in my stomach.

"When the boat docks we're going to the bank," I tell Hayden. "After that, we're going to find a place to stay."

"What about Mom?"

My reassuring smile fades. "We need to establish a home base first. He won't kill her. You know that."

Hayden doesn't really know it, not in the way that I do. But he nods anyway. I know that the man who has our mother wants to possess her. He won't kill her. Killing her would take away all that motivates him. Keeping my mother, owning her, was what kept him breathing and hunting. It also kept us running. No one could help us.

IT HAD ALL STARTED SO innocently. I remember my

mother telling me about it. It was before Hayden was born. I was about his age when I first started to understand that we were a little different from other families. It might have been earlier, but when you're not of school age, you don't mark time the same way. Seasons blend together and time seems to go on forever. No rituals divide the months. No back-to-school shopping. No carnivals. No winter breaks. I'm not even sure where we were living then, except I remember the smells of the country. Cow smells. A dairy farm was nearby. The land was flat, long, and green all the way to the edge of the horizon. Later, I learned we had been living in eastern Nebraska, not far from the Iowa border.

Mom was on the sofa talking to somebody on the phone. It wasn't a cell phone, but a landline that ran from the wall in the kitchen all the way to the living room. Her voice carried a sharp edge that brought me from my bedroom upstairs. She was crying. Seeing Mom cry made me cry too. I watched from the hallway. Something told me to stay put. Just listen.

" . . . what am I supposed to do now?" she was asking.

I moved a little closer, but still out of view. It was nighttime and I was wearing a pale yellow flannel nightgown. On my feet were slippers made to look like pink bunny rabbits. I loved those slippers more than anything. I never saw them again after that night.

" . . . tell me just how that's supposed to work?"

After a long silence, Mom hung up the phone. She stayed very still on the sofa and wrapped an old crocheted blanket around her shoulders.

I recall something else just then. *It was Christmas time*. Our tree was up next to the fireplace. Why hadn't I remembered this before?

I take my mind back to that place. I stood there frozen, watching Mom. I had the impulse to run over and hug her, but I was too scared. Later, when I thought about the reasons for my reluctance to interfere, I figured that it had to do with the fact that my mother was a private person. To see her crying almost seemed like a violation of her privacy.

Then she saw me. I felt a jolt go through my body. I was caught. She recovered a little and motioned for me to come closer. I followed the trajectory of her finger to a spot next to her on the sofa.

"Honey," she said, "I'm all right, but I do have something to tell you. It's about tomorrow. We're going to take a little trip tomorrow. It'll be fun."

Her eyes were red and nothing that came from her lips seemed like it could possibly be fun.

"Where?" I finally asked.

"That's the fun part," she said, trying to sound upbeat. "I don't know. *We* don't know." Her eyes left mine and wandered around the room. I followed them until her gaze stood still.

On our coffee table was a travel magazine with the image of a log cabin in the woods.

"We're going out West," she said.

Her random choice scared me. It felt desperate. "Why?"

But my mother had pulled herself together now. She was in full-on survival mode, an affectation that I later knew to be a complete façade. "Because we have to get away from someone. Someone bad. Someone who wants to hurt me."

I didn't understand exactly what she meant. But the funny thing about it was that I didn't even ask. I just accepted it. The next morning, I found her in front of the fireplace burning papers and photographs. I watched my own image get licked and then devoured by orange and blue flames.

Ten minutes later, we were gone and my name was no longer Shelly. We took nothing with us. Not even those pink bunny slippers. I always missed those slippers so much.

"Anna," she said, trying out my new name as we drove toward the highway, "starting over will save us. Starting over is the only way we can survive."

Chapter Five

Cash: $107.80.
*Food: Coffee and a maple bar for me, hot chocolate and a maple
bar for Hayden.*
Shelter: None at the moment.
Weapons: Same scissors.
Plan: Stay calm.

BEFORE WE LEAVE FOR THE bank, we make one more
stop. If I'm going to get into the safe deposit box, I'm going
to have to look like *her*. Mom. Her backup ID is in Dad's
wallet. My hair is pretty much Mom-ready right now. But my
clothes still look like a teenager's. A hoodie and jeans might
work, depending on the bank cashier's mood. I can fake her
latest signature no problem—she doesn't know that I've done
it a time or two to get out of speech class. It isn't that I mind
getting up in front of a group to give a speech on a subject, like
how social networking is driving people further apart and not
closer together. Or maybe a demonstration speech on how to
make fortune cookies with subversive messages like:

Holy crap! You're a loser.

You will never find love.

Your best moment was so five minutes ago.

I did that demo speech in January and got an A-minus. What I don't like are the impromptu speeches—the ones in which the teacher tells you to share a story from your childhood, to talk about family traditions that you value most. Or anything genuinely personal. I'm a good liar, but not to people that I see every day. I can lie to strangers without even the tiniest flutter of remorse.

I drag Hayden to the Lost and Found office in the ferry terminal at Colman Dock. It isn't open yet, so we sit and wait, mostly in silence. We watch people come and go. We also notice a homeless man with a garbage bag of cans. I hope we never end up like some sad soda-can forager.

Finally, a door opens and we pounce on a young man with a faint moustache and stubble on his chin behind the counter.

"Our mom left her jacket on the ferry the other day," I say, as if my inquiry is more out of boredom than urgency.

"Yeah, that's right," Hayden says.

I shoot him a look. This is *my* deal. My little brother is just supposed to keep his trap snapped shut.

The man catches my vibe and I give him what I know he wants.

"She'd forget *me* if she could," I say.

He nods. "Yeah, I have a mom like that too. Can you describe what it looks like?"

I shake my head. "Mom-boring. That's what it looks like. I'd know it if I see it."

"That's not the way it works. We have a lot of crap back

50

there. You have to tell me what it looks like."

"God," I say. "Dark, ugly. She just said she left it. I'll just tell her someone took it." I turn and start walking nonchalantly. Inside I'm waiting. I'm hoping.

"Hey," the man says. "It's against rules, but go ahead and look around."

"Really?" I say, a little relieved.

"I have to pee," Hayden says.

"Just a second," I answer.

"No. I can't wait."

"We'll never find that jacket. And Mom will yell at us. She's such a bitch to me."

The man looks at my brother. "I'll take him and stand outside and wait." He turns to me. "You look for the ugly-ass jacket."

I return the wry grin on Hayden's face. He's not so terribly awful after all. He can take direction. Even if he is a homeschooler.

The door shuts and I instantly feel like I'm in one of those shopping spree videos. I only have a few minutes to get what I need. I paw through the coats and jackets like a wild woman. I can easily see why no one came back for any of them. They're all totally Ross Dress-For-Less rejects. I find one, a black jacket from the Brass Plum that looks mommy-desperate enough. Next, I grab a bag. It's black leather with a fake Chanel clasp. It's the same purse Gemma had at the beginning of the school year. I wonder if she lost hers. I'll never see her again, so I guess none of that matters. It'll work better than my backpack, that's for sure. I find a cool graphic T-shirt for Hayden and wad it into a ball and stuff it in my new purse. My eyes scan the small room.

A white silk scarf. Stained. Gross. But it'll work. My heart is racing. I know I'm not on a game-show video, but I feel that kind of a rush. *Hurry! Ten seconds to go! You're running out of time!* I pick through the sunglasses— there are dozens of pairs in a big plastic tote next to the shoes. *Who loses their shoes on a ferry?* It seems like everyone whoever rode that ferry left their glasses aboard. I find a Kate Spade pair that might even be real. Those go in my new purse too.

The door opens and my brother and the Lost and Found guy are there.

"Looks like you found it," LFG says.

I nod with a sour look on my face. "Yeah. I'd know this anywhere. If my mom had any sense she'd have left it here. But no. It's her favorite jacket of all time."

LFG looks at me and nods. He pays no attention to the black leather purse which I slip casually over my shoulder as though it were mine.

Which it now is. Sort of.

THE BANK IS ON FIFTH Avenue and as I look I see a mix of the wealthy and the street people congregating around its big brass-framed doors. I know that Hayden and I fit in somewhere between the two factions vying for coffee, money, and whatever people in crisp, new suits think is important. A black mongrel,with a white spot under his chin that looks like he's just finished slurping up a bowl of milk, curls up next to a man. At his feet, facing the movers and shakers of that Seattle sidewalk, is a cardboard sign that says in crudely drawn letters:

You and me both, I think, as my little brother and I go inside.

Even though it is against my better judgement, I tell Hayden to wait on one of those black leather sofas next to the spires of a stiff green plant that looks like it could be a weapon—if I was really desperate.

Hayden is not to talk to anyone. Look at anyone. *Trust anyone.* Just stay put. My heart could not beat any faster if I'd had a gun in my pocket and had planned to actually rob the bank. Which, of course, isn't my mission. I wait in line with my mother's ID—the one that had my age at thirty-something. Part of me dreads that I could pass for someone that old, but the other part—the part that wants to survive and find my mother's captor—desires nothing more than to have the clerk look me over, think I'm my mother, so that I can retrieve whatever is so important from the vault.

I leave my stolen sunglasses on and I make sure my scarf is draped messily around my neck as though I was in a hurry. I *am* in a hurry. A hurry to get out of here as fast as I can.

The clerk, a young man with an X-acto blade-sharp nose and unibrow, looks over my ID and compares it with the signature card that he pulls from a file cabinet behind him. It seems like a very, very long time, but it was probably only a second. His hair is blond—golden, really. I wonder if my hair looks as bad as his.

"This doesn't look like you," he says curtly.

"I get that a lot," I answer in a throatier version of my voice, one that I assume sounds like my mother —or at least someone older than fifteen. I offer no excuse. Sometimes the less you say, the better the odds are of getting what you want.

"Did you change your hair or something?" he asks.

I shrug as if the remark doesn't challenge me, which it does. "I change my hair about three times a year, so . . . yeah, I changed my hair."

He raises his unibrow and I instantly think of a big, hairy McDonald's arch.

"Looks better the way it is now," he says.

I wonder if he's hitting on me and if he is, he is breaking the law. I am underage, no matter what that ID card states. At least I am pretty sure I am. I couldn't be eighteen. Or could I? I don't have time to pursue that thought now. It's creepy, but if this guy thinks I'm a woman and not a girl then I must be doing something right.

"Follow me," he says, dangling the vault key like a dog treat—not quite ready to give it to me, but reminding me how much is at stake and how he literally holds the key over my head. He's wearing corduroy trousers and as he walks he makes a swishing sound. I almost want to laugh, but I feel so scared and sick inside I think a laugh would just make me throw up.

He leads me over to a little iron gate at the end of the row of cashiers and unlocks it with a big flourish, eyeing me with a look I feel unsure about. *A leer? With suspicion?* I've seen looks like that before, but the teller's face shuts down like a sea anemone poked with the tip of a clam digger's shovel and I'm unsure about what he's thinking. *Maybe about his job? Maybe he caught that unibrow in the reflection of the tellers' booths and finally realizes he has to do something about it?* I follow him to the safe deposit room, down a tiled corridor that is impressively bleak.

He stops at the doorway and turns to face me.

"Passcode?"

"What?" I ask, my pulse quickening.

"You need to enter your passcode," he says, his eyes riveted to mine.

I feel sweat collect on the back of my neck. Passcode? I don't have any passcode. His nicotine stained index finger points at a keypad.

"I thought all I needed was my box key," I say, running every memory through my mind that could lead to a passcode. I knew the code Dad had left in blood meant to get away. But a passcode for a safe deposit box?"

"I have a passkey and you need to give me your personal passcode," he says. "We need both to enter the vault."

I think hard and fast. Now my face is hot. It must be red. Great. Nothing's coming to me and I think Unibrow knows it.

He shifts his weight. "If you don't have the passcode, you can't go inside," he says.

"I'm having a brain freeze," I say, really hating this guy right now. "So many passwords to remember."

"We haven't got all day," he says, turning to go back down the corridor.

I punch the numbers for my birthday—at least the date that I think it is.

Nothing.

Think. Think.

"You only have three chances and if you don't get it right

we'll need to arrange for the bank manager to create you a new one. He's a real stickler for security around here."

I know I'll like the bank manager even less than Unibrow, who by the way, is now in my personal top five of all annoying people. Number one is Miley Cyrus.

I punch in my brother's birthday. Again, nothing. Don't parents routinely use their kids' birthdays for such things? We don't have a dog, so using an animal's name isn't going to be it.

"Let's go see the manager," he says. A slight smile on his face indicates that he's happy that I can't remember the code. He must want to go on a smoke break, because he smells like an ashtray to me.

Then it comes to me. My mind flashes to the day that my mom and dad set up the router for our internet connection. The password they used was the same one they used on everything— whenever anything required some kind of security code.

"Wait!" I say. "I have it."

My finger goes to the keypad and I hit the following letters and numbers *LY4E1234.*

Love you forever and a digit for each member of our family.

Stupid me. Mom told me over and over that our family password for our router, security system, even internet shopping account was always the same.

A green light flickers on the keypad display. I let out a very quiet sigh of relief.

Unibrow looks me over and inserts his passkey. And he leads me inside. It's a surprisingly large space with row upon row of shiny brass-fronted drawers. A table fills the center space. Three beams of light fall on its glossy black surface.

He looks in my direction but I pay no attention.

Instead, my eyes scan for Box 2443, the number on the key. I insert the little brass key and the box is released from the wall. I'm not really sure what's inside it, but my parents have told me that everything I need is there.

"All righty then," Unibrow says. "I'll leave you to your box. Buzz me when you want to get out of our little prison."

He says the words with a smile and I know it is supposed to be a joke that he uses all the time. But I don't return his attempt at humor with a smile or anything that resembles a lighthearted response. Instead, my eyes stick like a magnet to steel on an envelope—the first of many filling the box.

On the outside of the large white envelope is an inscription in my mother's handwriting.

For my daughter's eyes only.

I quickly notice that there is a second envelope with another recipient in mind.

For my son's eyes only.

I wonder if this is in case I'm taken or killed. It sends a current of uneasiness through my body. I know without any uncertainty that my mom and my stepdad had considered I might be a casualty of their choices, their lives. I open the first envelope, the one marked for me—and my eyes only. I'll save Hayden's for another time. I can barely breathe. My stomach is the nest of snakes in the bottom of that pit in the old Indiana Jones DVD that Hayden made me watch at least eight hundred times. Dad is dead. Murdered. Mom is missing. And for some reason I'm expecting to find answers—and comfort—in the contents of a letter.

Inside is yet another envelope, imprinted with a warning.

Do not read this in front of the bank employees. There is a camera in the corner of the room. Turn your back to the camera before you read any more.

I know my mother very, very well. She doesn't want anyone to see my reaction. She wants me to protect myself. I slowly turn away from the steady red light of the camera. For the first time, I notice how cold the air is in that hermetically sealed room. I shiver as I find my fingertips under the flap of the envelope. I tear it open.

Honey,

If you are reading the letter then I am gone. As I write this I don't know what exactly that might really mean. It is one of two possibilities. He has captured me or he has killed me. I know you will want to find out where I am, if I'm alive. I know that I cannot stop you from doing so. I am sorry that there is very little here to tell you where I might be. I have put some information into some other envelopes. I want you to take those along with this when you leave. Do not show any of it to anyone. If you do, not only will I die, you probably will too. Please sit down. There is a chair on the other side of this room.

I stop reading and drag the black leather chair closer to the gleaming black table with the open safe deposit box. One wheel is stuck and the chair refuses to go in a straight line. My knees feel a little weak and I'm grateful for the chair as I slide into its icy cushions. I feel that shiver once more and I shake it off. I want to thank Mom, as though her letter is part of a conversation. But it isn't. It is a message, a request. Maybe an edict. I won't know unless I read on. I don't want to, though. It's like I'm in a car, driving past the worst, bloodiest car accident ever. I know that what I'll see will freak me out, shock me forever.

My mother doesn't disappoint.

Honey, I have lied to you. I didn't mean for my lies to spin out of control and frame so much of our lives. You have to believe me when I say that being a liar isn't what I set out to be. I lied because it was the only course of action to save you, save me, save Hayden. I used to think that by ignoring the truth just maybe a little of my nightmare would go away. Pay attention to my words and remember the need for forgiveness. It is real. It is the only way to salvation.

The man who we have been running from our entire lives was not a jilted boyfriend. Not a stalker. At least not the kind of stalker that you—or I—could ever imagine. I felt as though you only needed to know a part of the story. You were so young when I started telling you the story, that I knew you would believe it. Two words here. Forgiveness and strength. For you to survive you must embrace both.

MY MIND RACES BACK TO a conversation my mother and I

had when I was around eleven. Maybe twelve. We were sitting outside on the back patio watching fireflies as they zipped through the lowest hanging branches of a big oak that spread over our entire backyard like it was protecting us. I loved that tree so much. When we moved that time, I vowed I'd live in a place again someday with a tree that had branches that functioned like caring arms. That afternoon a news story came on TV talking about a gun battle between members of a cult and law enforcement authorities. It stayed on my mind well past dinner.

"Sometimes I feel like those kids on TV," I said.

Mom looked at me, the light from the flame of a small citronella candle playing off her beautiful, even features.

"What do you mean?" she asked.

"The cult kids," I said a little tentatively. Not because I felt tentative about what I was saying, but because I felt like I was lighting a fuse. "They are born into something. Their parents wanted to be a part of something. They didn't have a choice."

She looked at me with those penetrating eyes of hers, and then returned her attention to the fireflies and our beloved oak tree.

"Honey, you feel that way too?" she asked. There was remorse in her voice, but not too much. Just a hint of regret. In some ways that was all I ever wanted from her. I wanted her to tell me that she was sorry our lives had been so screwed up. That she shouldered some of the blame. Even if she didn't, really.

"Sometimes," I lied. I felt that way all the time. My mother's choices had dragged me into a life that left me without any history of my own. I tried not to resent her, because I loved her so much. Yet, there were times when I just hated her for what she'd done to me, and to Hayden. As I grew older, I sometimes allowed myself to see her side of things. The reasons why she did what she did. My mother's story was flimsy, but since she told it with such evasive conviction, I never really questioned it.

WHILE THOSE MEMORIES ATTACK MY brain with the ferocity of a thousand ice picks, I try to focus. I shake my head as if to free myself from a firestorm of nerves and questions. I need to concentrate on the letter. My heart rate is going faster. I look down on the paper and a tear drops on it. It leaves a shiny pool on the letter that I notice for the first time is written in pencil. I'm almost afraid to read on. I'm worried that her words will break my heart, that the betrayal she's hinting at will be too great.

We've been running our whole lives from your father. It makes me ill to put those words to paper, but that's the truth.

My father? My father was dead. He was an army enlistee who died in Iraq. I have carried his picture in my wallet for as long as I've had one. I have another reminder. I press my fingertips against the dog tags that hang around my neck on a silver, braided chain that I'd saved up to buy from the Macy's jewelry counter in Minneapolis.

The first tag has his name, enlistment number, and blood type.

Walters, William J
FG123456Z
A Neg

On the second one was the next of kin:

Ginger Walters
1337 Maple Lane
Tacoma, WA

For a moment anger and confusion well up as my emotions battle for some kind of strange supremacy. I have no idea where this is going, so I read on. I take in the last words in big, oxygen-free gulps.

What I have to tell you does not define who you are. Not at all. You are my beautiful daughter. I have done everything I can to spare you the reality of your conception. But you are here reading this and you deserve to know the truth. You also can decide if you want to help me. If you don't, I will die loving you anyway. If you don't, please take care of your brother. Take him to my sister Ginger Rhodes' place in Wallace, Idaho, and leave him there until after you are sure I am safe or dead. Your birth father will never harm him.

This is too much. *Sister? Ginger—the name on the dog tags?* I'm reeling now. We had no family. We never did. Mom said that her parents and siblings died in a car crash when she was a little girl. Seven, I think. Though now I am beginning to question everything I thought I knew. And as I do, my eyes take in a sentence that no one should have to read.

Your father is Alex Richard Rader. He is a serial killer. I was the victim who got away.

I want to scream, but I don't. Tears stream down my face and I half-glance at the bank's camera trained right at me. I feel scared, paranoid and very, very angry. The words feel toxic. *Serial killer? Victim? Got away?* Each syllable comes at me like bullets to my temple. I almost wish they were bullets. All of a sudden my skin feels dirty and itchy. My hands are shaking. I am feeling such loathing for my mother. She could have told me. She *should* have told me. She made our vagabond lives utter hell. Why didn't she just go to the police? She had always said that her stalker was an ex-boyfriend, a man who had come into her life after my father—who now I know wasn't my father at all—died in Iraq. She'd been kind to him and he just wouldn't let up. We were living in military housing in Fort Lewis, south of Tacoma, back then. I was barely out of diapers. She said that the military police refused to do anything to help her, that her stalker hadn't broken any laws. And yet she felt so threatened that she thought that being on the run was the only solution for our safety. I want to laugh out loud now about the absurdity of her story, but she'd been so unbelievably convincing. Every time a freak would stalk and kill someone when a restraining order had been put in place, she would point to it as an example of the world we lived in—and the danger of living life out in the open.

"No one can help a victim until it is too late. It's a chance we're never going to take," she'd said on those occasions.

I bought into it. I guess the drumming of the same thing over and over ensured my complete acceptance. Like those cult kids we had seen on TV years ago. They had no other frame of reference for the world. They believed everything their leaders told them. Even when the stories were stretched to the breaking point, they still believed.

I know what I know, honey. So please give me that. I know that Alex has killed three girls and those cases were never truthfully solved. I also know why. I know that his friends on the police force tampered with evidence. I know all of this because he told me when he held me captive when I was sixteen. I could draw you a picture about what happened during those dark days, but I don't think I need to. You were conceived in the worst horror imaginable. But I would never want to live without you. I don't see him when I look into your eyes. I see the face of the daughter that I will always love.

If you decide to try to find me alive—I know I can't stop you—you will need to follow his trail. I don't know where he is. I don't know where I am. But I do know two things. I have seven days. He killed each girl after holding them for seven days. A week. Look into the victims' pasts to find me.

I look down at the pages and I see photographs cut from various newspapers. Though the images have yellowed with age, any one of them could have been a ringer for my mother. Shannon Blume, sixteen; Megan Moriarty, sixteen; Leanne Delmont, sixteen. All were from the Seattle-Tacoma area. All of these murder cases were attributed to different men. All cases were closed. According to the newspaper clippings, none of the names who killed any of the girls was Alex Rader.

What was my mother talking about?

I don't get it. I don't really get any of this. I gather everything up. Most of the envelopes are flat, a few contain some bulges. I feel one of them and the bulge has shape that I instantly know. I take my fingers off as though they've been burned. My brain creates a picture of what I felt and adrenaline nearly causes me to pass out. A shockwave of fear runs through me.

I stuff all the envelopes and loose papers into the purse I stole from the Lost and Found office at the ferry terminal on Colman Dock. I take a deep, calming breath. My brain is cycling over and over. Trying to pull my thoughts together is harder than anything I've ever done. I'm on information overload and I know it.

You can do this. Who your parents are doesn't define you, I lie to myself.

I push the button.

A moment later, the locks tumble and Unibrow enters the now utterly airless room.

"Finished?" he asks as if my standing there ready to go isn't enough of a clue.

"I think so," I mutter as I move my purse closer to my body, holding it tight. Never letting it go, even though its contents frighten me in every way imaginable.

He looks down at the empty safe deposit box. "Are you closing out the account?"

For a nanosecond, I'm unsure exactly what he said. My mind is elsewhere. "No. Not at all."

I watch him put it back into the one gaping hole in the wall of boxes and I sign the document he's set on the black table with my mother's name.

A minute later, I'm in the lobby retrieving Hayden from the black leather chair that had held him like a playpen.

"Hey," he says. "What was in there?"

I don't look at him.

"Nothing. A big zero."

He knows that I've been crying, but he doesn't say a thing about it.

"Where are we going now? To the police?"

I take his hand, which now feels so very small, and I pull him toward the sunlight of the street. "No. We're going to our aunt's in Idaho."

He looks at me with those eyes of his. "What aunt?"

So much has been crammed into my head, a mass of loose ends that feel like they've coagulated inside my throat, that I really can't speak. Instead, I jerk him down the street. Into a crowd of people hurrying to things that they know. A lunch date with a friend, a business meeting, a store in which they will shop.

My brother and I are hurrying into a very dark unknown.

And in one of the envelopes I have a gun.

THE KING STREET STATION IS just south of Pioneer Square, the city's eclectic historic district with homeless and runaway teens fighting for corner space. I fit in there, I know. But I don't intend to stay. And while I'm not sure about what I am going to do, I know of only one place to go.

"Two tickets to Wallace, Idaho," I say to the clerk behind the glass partition at the railroad station's ticket window.

"The line goes as far as Spokane. You will have to transfer

66

to a bus for Wallace."

I pay for the tickets, leaving us only a few dollars. I'll need to do something about that. Hayden has been bugging me nonstop for information about what was in the safe deposit box. I tell him only bits and pieces. I don't tell him how much of a liar our mother was. I don't tell him that I'm so hurt and angry that I only want to find her so that I can yell at her.

"We have relatives in Idaho. We're going there to stay. We'll be safe."

"Idaho? What relatives?" he asks excitedly, seemingly missing the point that up to that moment our parents have fed us a pack of lies.

"Mom has a sister. Apparently."

We take a seat in the back of the second car. I let Hayden have the window. He's tired and I'm hoping the monotonous beat of a rolling train will lull him to sleep. A woman in front of us is looking at the newspaper and I pray that it isn't the same one we saw on the ferry that morning. The rhythm and rumble of the wheels against the track do precisely what I knew they'd do. Hayden's asleep.

I pull out the envelopes and papers from the safe deposit box and consume the information on each page as if I were a human scanner. I am, sort of. I've always had the ability to remember things. I know that I possess a photographic memory. I never say so aloud. It sounds too conceited, but I do. And yeah, maybe sometimes, I guess I am a little conceited too. While I'm taking everything inside, while I'm feeling the gun in its paper wrapper, I'm thinking. I'm thinking over and over about what is happening to Mom. I am so mad at her for the lies she's told me. I feel foolish too. I imagined the father I never knew, the soldier, and how he'd fought for our country. He was a hero. When I was little I used to pretend that I was talking to him on the phone all the way across the world. He was dodging bullets, bombs. He was facing death inside some burned-out village in the Middle East, but he stopped everything to talk to me. I saw my father as a kind of superhero worthy of respect, love, and a movie. All of that was a figment of my imagination.

My stepfather was a good guy. Decent. Yet still a mystery. Why would he take us on? There had to be something wrong with a man who would carry such a burden as to live on the run with my mother, me, and later, Hayden. I loved him in the way that one loves a trusted pet, one who might bite you, so you never get too close. He was solid. Caring. But he wasn't my dad. He was Hayden's dad. My stomach roils as I think of him nearly pinned to the floor of the kitchen with a knife, like some moth specimen in Biology class at South Kitsap. I want to cry for him right now. He deserves that much, but I can't.

I can't think of anything but my bio dad and who he was. He was not dog-tag material. He was not the hero. Far, far from that. He was the villain, the worst, most despicable kind ever. The feeling that overtakes me right now as Hayden sleeps in the seat next to me is a mix of sadness, anger, and confusion. If I'm not the daughter of a hero, but the daughter of a killer, then what kind of person am I? Hayden stirs and I feel the gun once more and look out the window as the forest blurs into one big smear of green.

Chapter Six

Cash: $30.00.
Food: Sandwiches (stale) on the train.
Shelter: The train, I guess.
Weapons: Gun, cheap scissors.
Plan: Find Mom and kill Dad.

A LITTLE MORE THAN AN hour later the bus from Spokane drops us in downtown Wallace, a historic mining town that looks movie-set ready. In fact, it had been the location of a movie about a volcano that decimated the town. Mom likes disaster movies. My life right now is a disaster, so it's fitting. It's late in the morning, about ten a.m. and I feel grungy from wearing the same clothes for more than two days. My stomach grumbles and I press the heel of my palm into my belly to quiet things down. I wait for Hayden outside the bus station's bathroom, making sure that no one goes in and no one comes out. I need to keep track of my brother.

A woman with kind brown eyes working at the snack bar gives directions to our aunt's place from an address provided by my thinking-ahead mother. We only have to make two lefts and a right. It can't be that bad. I thank the woman and try to commit the directions to memory.

"It's quite a ways," she says. "You need a ride?"

I see the look on her face and I know that she's wary and concerned. She watched me linger by the bathroom and she knows my brother and I are traveling alone. I don't want to stand out, but with my overly blond, slept-in hair, I imagine that blending in isn't something that is even remotely possible. As far as Idaho goes, I bet I look pretty edgy.

"We'll manage," I say, dodging her direct gaze as I peel a *Historic Mining Town* map from the rack by the bathroom. Her simple directions are now eluding me. I have too much to think about right now.

"Hey," Hayden says, coming out of the bathroom, his zipper in need of a pull, "I want a ride."

I give him a look. "No. No we don't. We're fine." I point to his zipper and his face turns a scary shade of crimson. It shuts him up, and that's good.

"Can I call someone for you?" the concerned woman asks.

I shake my head. "Ah, no. Our dad's friend is supposed to pick us up." I say *friend* because I think it'll stop her from asking who our father is. We don't have one. Hayden doesn't for sure. And I do, but I intend to kill him.

"I see," she says.

Now I know by the tone in her voice that what she really sees are two strangers, young strangers, in town. She sees trouble.

And so do I. My guard is up. Way up. I feel like I'm an armadillo and I've rolled up into a little ball and I'm not going to let anyone inside. Not even a crack.

70

"Hey," I say, looking out in front at a rusted white Bronco parked across the street. "Dad's friend is here."

I pull Hayden for the door, because I'm pretty sure he's stupid enough to say that Dad—*his* dad—is in the Port Orchard morgue on a table with a forensic pathologist wielding a bone saw.

But he isn't as stupid as I think.

"That was close," he says. "Is there a Starbucks?"

I sigh. "You're seven and you don't drink coffee. And no there isn't. Look around you. We're in Idaho, for God's sake, Hayden."

He doesn't care. "I'm hungry."

"You're always hungry." I fish a granola bar from the bottom of the purse and hand it to him. I take another for myself. As we crunch away on the sidewalk in front of the station, I am reminded of the small town where we lived when I first had the feeling, finally caught on that Mom and I weren't like others in the neighborhood.

I think I was three, maybe four. A neighbor lady came to our door. Behind her was a pretty little girl with green eyes and red hair. She was shy, sweet. Although I was drawn to her, I hung back behind my mother's legs.

The woman said something about her daughter wanting to play with me. Just the words made me feel excited. I was always alone. Me and Mom.

"I'm sorry," Mom said, "but my little girl is sick. She's got the chicken pox. Very contagious."

I didn't know I was sick.

After the lady and the girl left, Mom must have noticed my confusion.

71

"We can't trust anyone, honey. No one. Do you understand?"

I didn't understand of course. All I knew was that I wanted to play with that girl, but Mom said I couldn't. Later, not long after, I'd learn that we were never to get close to anyone. I never did. Not until I was named Rylee. I met a boy at South Kitsap. If I'd been a normal girl, with a normal family, I think things might have gone further. We never really went out. I couldn't do that. We talked in the cafeteria or on the track. He was a runner too. He has the most beautiful eyes and a way of making me feel special. Just with a look.

I know that I can never call Caleb. I can never see him again. I wonder what he's thinking right now. If I'm on his mind the same way he's on mine?

I think about that time we really talked for the first time.

The time his hand touched mine.

CALEB HUNTER WAS WEARING A T-shirt with a mangled cross that stretched across his chest. I wondered if he was being ironic or if I should say I was a Christian too. I've been Catholic and even Jewish, but only in name. I'm not sure what I am when it comes to the category of faith. But I was sure that I liked Caleb Hunter.

"This school sucks," he said, his eyes looking right into mine. It was a searing look, and for some reason, I turned away.

Even with the most innocuous statements or questions, Caleb seemed to have that kind of effect on me. Like he was reading me. I allow myself the fantasy that he liked what he was reading, but I'm not a good judge of what others really think. I assume most are as deceptive as I've been.

"Yeah," I said, agreeing with him. Actually, I was glad to be there. It beat my prison sentence of sitting at the kitchen table-classroom with Mom and Hayden.

It was the first time we had really talked. It started with the trivial, about how we didn't like someone—the poseurs that make up most of the upper class—and how we couldn't wait to get a driver's license. He said he was getting his any time now.

"I'm jealous," I said.

"Yeah. I can get out of here and leave this town and my dad and his girlfriend and never, ever come back."

I know that his mother had died that summer. I could see the despair in the way he hung his shoulders as he sat in front of me in Washington State History.

"I'm sorry about your mom," I said, allowing my eyes to look into his for as long as I could manage, without being weird.

"Thanks. Dad doesn't want to talk about it and, of course, that bitch he's about to marry doesn't either."

I didn't know what else to say, so his words hung in the air.

"Rylee, have you ever just wanted to disappear?" he finally asked.

I had to lie again. The truth is that I've been disappearing all of my life. I was finally beginning to feel like I had a home. Part of that was the boy I was sitting with now.

"Totally," I said.

He looked toward the window and out to the parking lot. "Sometimes I just want to fill up my backpack and leave. For good." He hesitated a little, looking at me. Measuring my response to his words.

I merely nodded.

"If you could go anywhere," he said, "do you know where it would be?"

I've been a lot of places, but nowhere that *I* wanted to be.

"Paris," I said. "But not the one in Texas. The one in France."

He broke out in a big smile. "I figured that out."

The bell rang and we both got up. As we parted in the direction of our classes—he was in Algebra, I was in Computer Science—his hand touched mine.

It sent a volt of energy through me. I didn't know if it was on purpose or if it had been an accident.

As my little brother and I make our way through the streets of Wallace, I can still feel Caleb's touch on the back of my hand.

GINGER RHODES, OUR NEWFOUND AUNT, lives at 244 Moon Gulch Road. The sun shines in our faces and Hayden and I squint in the direction we must go. I still don't know what I'll say to Aunt Ginger, or if I can even call her that with a straight face. Or without bursting out in tears. I wonder if she knows about me and Hayden. After all, we didn't know about *her*.

We stand outside like garden statues looking at her house, a gray and blue two-story tucked into the base of a ridge that runs down from the mountains. Old. But in decent repair. I'm grateful that it isn't a leaky old mobile home. I'd seen an episode of *Dr. Phil* in which some kids went looking for their birth parents only to find out they were living in a rusted out trailer on some riverbank somewhere. The kids on the show had decided that their adoptive parents weren't so bad after all. Sometimes you have to be grateful for what you have. I have nothing but Hayden, and I know that I should continue to find more good things about that.

I take a deep breath and knock on the bright, yield-sign-yellow door. I feel scared and nervous.

The yellow door opens and a face that looks like mine, one that looks like my mother, appears through the wire mesh of the screen door.

"Yes?" the woman behind the door says. She is about my height. Her hair is long, not Mormon-sister-wife long, but close to that. A thick strand hangs over her shoulder. She is wearing jeans and a Wallace High School T-shirt.

"Are you Ginger Rhodes?"

She nods, looking us over. "Yes. Are you here about the daffodil bulbs?"

I swallow hard. "No. I think you're my aunt." I pull Hayden closer. "*Our* aunt."

Her light blue eyes narrow and I watch her eyelids flutter. She looks around the street, her yard, the driveway, and opens the screen door, tentatively. She licks her lips nervously before she says anything.

"Hurry inside," she says as the screen door slams, and the yellow front door shuts behind us.

We're not there to deliver daffodil bulbs, but rather some very bad news. Aunt Ginger, if this is her, knows it. Aunt Ginger knows *us*.

The hallway is dark, a bright light from the windows on the other side of the house pools at our feet.

"Where is Courtney?" she asks, her voice spiking with emotion.

"He's got her," I say, testing her, this new aunt of mine.

And then she does something that I couldn't have imagined, something that no one other than my parents has ever done. Aunt Ginger hugs me. I don't know why for sure, but tears start streaming down my face. I don't know who this lady is, not really. But I melt into her arms and I cry harder than I ever have since the ordeal began. I can cry loudly because I feel that someone cares and that even though I'm in a stranger's place, I'm with family. I drop my purse to the floor. Hayden awkwardly puts his arms around me too and he cries. She cries. It is not a reunion of joy, but something completely different. We are a sobbing mass of pain, loss and fear.

"He took your mother," Aunt Ginger says. "Didn't he?"

I can barely speak. My throat feels as if someone is squeezing it shut. "Yes, and he killed our father," I finally say, the words making me cry even harder.

I don't say *Hayden's* father, because my little brother has enough to deal with. He doesn't need to know that his world has been shifted on its axis and is never going to spin the way it did before we found that hunting knife in our father's chest. *Hayden's father's* chest.

Aunt Ginger pulls away a little. She doesn't let go completely, but just enough so that she can see our faces.

"Is Courtney dead too?"

It is weird to hear her say my mother's name. *Her real name.* Not the one engraved on the dog tags around my neck. My mother's name wasn't Ginger. Ginger is my aunt.

"I don't know," I say. "I don't think so."

"The creep took her," Hayden adds.

Aunt Ginger runs her hand over her weeping eyes and leads

us away from the door, but not without turning the deadbolt first, and hooking up a brass-colored chain. She's taking no chances. She directs us into the living room, but not without first shutting the curtains that run along the entire expanse of windows. Like a floodlight burned out, the pool of sunlight on the floor is gone. We sit on the sofa, the TV on mute. A coffee cup is on the table. Aunt Ginger was living her life, doing what she always did, and we just walked in and took it over. While she is obviously distressed, she didn't react as I would have expected.

She wasn't shocked.

She fumbles around, trying to think of the right thing to say. I expect that there is no right thing. We've been kept away from her for our entire lives and she went along with it. I want to be kind. I want to think that all of this has been for our own good, but I'm not sure. The betrayal is deep, and apparently, shared.

"The last time I saw your mother . . . last Labor Day . . . she told me that she thought you'd have to move again soon. She thought he was closing in on her. I told her that she was paranoid, you know, more paranoid than cautious. I told her to stay put. I told her that his threats would never evolve into reality. I . . . "

Aunt Ginger is shaking as she speaks. She's falling apart. I don't want to confront her right now, but really? *Really?* Did she see our mother last Labor Day? Did this aunt who we never knew existed up until twenty-four hours ago stay in touch with our mother, and nobody bothered to tell us?

"Are you really our mom's sister?" says Hayden, whose mind

is obviously going to the same place as mine.

She manages a smile and directs it at him. "Older sister. Yes, I am."

"Do we have any other aunts and uncles?" he asks. "Do we have cousins?"

Aunt Ginger wipes her eyes again, leaving a trail of mascara on her sleeve. "No other aunts and uncles. But yes, I have a son and daughter," she says. "I don't see them . . . often."

Again, I'm stunned. At this point, however, I wonder why I should be? My mother lied about her sister. She lied about my real father, for years. Why not lie about everyone else in the family?

Aunt Ginger offers us food and drink. Hayden takes her up on the offer, but I don't.

"Aunt Ginger," I say, "do you know where my . . . where he took Mom?"

She shakes her head no.

"Do you know where he lives?"

Again, no.

"Are you going to help us find Mom?"

Aunt Ginger hesitates. "Let's figure it out later."

"There is no later," I say in the most direct way that I can.

She bites down on her lower lip before speaking. "I mean, after you eat and rest."

I don't understand her peculiar reluctance. *Her sister has been abducted by a serial killer. Why is she being so weird?*

Hayden's eyes have landed on a cheese sandwich and a stack of Pringles potato chips that Aunt Ginger has set on two denim-blue plates that she's placed on an enormous table in the kitchen. On the wall adjacent to the table are some photographs. Lots of them. My heart skips a beat and I feel a surge of bewilderment. My school photo is among a bunch of images of complete strangers. There's an old picture of Hayden, too. We were part of a family. We just didn't know it.

Aunt Ginger turns to me and mouths some words.

"After he's in bed, we'll talk then."

I sit down across from my brother while our aunt pours milk from a carton. I don't even like milk, but I say nothing. I sit there thinking of how the forces have collided to make my life worse than it has ever been.

And how my mother has less than six days to stay alive if I don't do something about it.

Chapter Seven

Cash: $24.50.
Food: Not an issue.
Shelter: A spare bedroom in our aunt's house in Idaho.
Weapons: Gun, crapola scissors, ice pick from kitchen.
Plan: The same. Find Mom. Kill Dad.

HAYDEN IS ASLEEP IN A bedroom across the hall from mine. The house on Moon Gulch Road is so quiet I can actually hear the clock in the foyer ticking away the time. If it has a loud chime, I will creep downstairs after midnight and stop it. I am a light sleeper and I think that tonight will be one for the record books. My mind has been racing, looping, spinning, since we arrived in Idaho. I don't know what I'm going to find out, but I know that whatever it is, it will change me. I peek in on my brother, but I don't go inside his room. His cheeks are pink and he's sleeping hard, which makes me feel just a little bit lighter. I hope that his dreams take him far away from what we've been through since everything happened.

I pad downstairs and find Aunt Ginger in the darkened living room, the curtains still drawn. The TV is still on mute.

The light flickering over her face alters her appearance a little. She doesn't look like my mother at all. Her eyes are darker, her hair is long and lifeless, without even the faintest trace of a shimmer. By the time I take a seat next to her, I had learned everything I could about her by studying all the photographs in the hallway, and yes, digging through every drawer that I could when she was getting our rooms ready. I know that she is single. She loves the scent of lavender. I know that she is estranged from her son and daughter. I don't exactly know why, and when it gets right down to it, I really don't care. What I do care about is the truth. What I care about is finding my mother.

"What happened to my mom?" I ask.

"What happened to her?" Aunt Ginger repeats my question, her expression confused. Or pretending to be confused. "Didn't you tell me he took her?"

I'm not going to fall for that stall tactic.

"Not now. *Back then*," I say. We both know what I'm getting at. But I let it slide.

Aunt Ginger gets up from the sofa, leaving me all alone, nearly swallowed up by its dark brown, velvet fabric. She keeps her face away from me, to the wall, but I can see it reflected on the glass of a framed picture. She is searching for the right words and I know that it has to be difficult.

It is for me too.

"When I was twenty, your mom was sixteen," she begins. "She was coming home from feeding the neighbor's cat. It was summer and the dahlias were in bloom. We had planned to go out shoppping after dinner. She needed a new outfit for a party at the end of the month." Aunt Ginger hesitates, lost in

81

a memory that must be bittersweet and horrific at the same time. I give her a minute. I have memories like that too; the kind that take me far away from the present.

"No one saw it happen," she says, back from wherever her thoughts have taken her. "I mean, she just vanished. It was as if Courtney was just lifted up away from home by a helicopter or something. There was no trace of her. Nothing."

She pauses, her face darkening as she goes back in time. She stops. I prod her. "What happened?"

Again, Aunt Ginger weighs how much she'll say. I want it all, but she looks at me and sees a kid. She has no idea how much strength I have or what I would do for my family. What I'd do even for her.

"How much do you know?" she finally asks.

I slide to the edge of the sofa. "I know who my real father is, if that's what you're asking."

Aunt Ginger spins around. Her long almost-sister-wife hair swings behind her like a pulled curtain. There is a look on her face that I can only describe as relief. Her eyes study mine for some deeper connection, some meaning. She nods at me.

"I'm sorry," she says.

I want to say something off the cuff, something flippant, to defuse how I really feel. I don't want her to know that I've imagined my DNA being made up of serial-killer genetic matter, a ladder of code that only leads to violence and murder. But I don't.

"What happened to her?" I persist.

"Your mom had been abducted by a monster. That's what happened."

"Besides getting her pregnant, what did he do? I have to know what you know if I'm going to find her."

She shakes her head. "Sweetheart. You're not going to find her."

Again, she clearly doesn't know me. She doesn't know what I'd do for someone in my family. She doesn't have a family. She's all alone. She's not a fighter. I am.

"Because she's already dead?" I ask, serving up the only concern I really have. If she's dead, I can't find her. Save her. Tell her how much I need her.

Tell her how pissed I am that she lied to me about everything.

Aunt Ginger returns to the brown velvet sofa. "No, no, not that. Because your mother wouldn't want you to."

"I'm not going to just let her die," I say, now wondering how this woman, my mother's own sister, could have any inkling of what my mother would want me to do. My mother expects a lot of me. She left me and Hayden alone with a bunch of clues. She wants me to try and find her.

I look over at the stolen purse, slumped by the front door where I dropped it when we first came inside. I consider retrieving it and pulling out the letters to show Aunt Ginger exactly what Mom told me to do. I think of the gun too. I hold back on those things.

"Look. I'm not a kid. Tell me everything. I have a right to know."

Aunt Ginger's hands tremble a little and I touch them. They feel cold. Bone cold. "Right. You do. It's just that it's so hard. So hard to talk about."

I nod because I understand, but there's a life at stake here.

"Start," I say. "Tell me everything."

Aunt Ginger inhaled half the oxygen in the room. "Your mom said she stopped to help someone who was trying to load some things into the back of a truck. The things weren't heavy, she told me later. Just awkward. Your mom is like that. Always helping people. When she wasn't looking, he came from behind her and put something over her mouth. Chloroform, she thinks. It could have been something else . . . "

My face doesn't give away how I'm feeling. "Go on," I manage to say. "What happened after she was taken?"

At first Aunt Ginger looks in the direction of the flickering images of the silent TV, but I can tell that she's not really watching it. I let her take another moment. Reliving whatever happened to Mom is painful for her. I get that.

She starts slowly. The words pummeling me: *captive*, *abused*, *tortured*. She tells me that my mother was subjected to the vilest of humiliations. She says that only the sickest, most depraved mind could conceive of the things done to her. Now that she started, it all comes tumbling out, and my aunt seems to be in another, horrifying world, until her eyes focus back on mine, realizing who I am. How old I am.

She stops. "You wanted to hear this, right?"

A long lapse hangs in the air.

"Of course. I said I did."

She stares at me with her penetrating eyes. She wants me to understand this next part, to embrace it.

"A weaker person would have folded and given up," she says. "But Courtney is the bravest girl that ever lived."

I wonder how she could say that. We've been on the run

my entire life. Exactly how is hiding brave?

"How did she get away?" I ask when she takes another pause from reliving the nightmare.

Aunt Ginger swallows and looks me in the eye. We are holding hands now. Hers no longer feel like ice.

"She said she was able to drug his coffee. She doesn't even know what the pills she used were. She should have cut his throat while she had the chance. It was the biggest mistake of her life. She regretted it more than anyone could ever know. She said she was too weak to kill him, no matter what he'd done to her."

"Why didn't she just go to the police and have him arrested?"

"Look, I can see you don't really understand. Not every criminal is caught. Not every victim is believed."

"I know that, but I still don't understand. It's worth a try, right?"

"Your mother *did* file a report. And she had her body probed and scraped for evidence. She said it was nearly as humiliating as what he'd done to her. She even told me once that she felt the police and the doctors were almost an extension of her captor's crimes. Their questions were like acid poured over her wounds. They didn't think that she had been abused, raped, whatever. Our mother—your grandmother—didn't believe her. Even I wondered about it."

"But why didn't anyone believe her?"

"Because she'd been captured once before." A pause. "Or she said she was."

Now I am confused. Completely.

"The year before she was raped," she goes on, "your mother

disappeared. She claimed she'd been kidnapped, but, well . . . "

I can tell by the way she's wringing her hands that this part is hard for her to disclose. The torture of my mother was, oddly, easier. "She'd run off to be with a boy. She had gone to the coast. She was afraid she would get in trouble so she made up a story."

My aunt sees the look on my face and she pounces. "She *was* kidnapped. She *was* brutalized by that monster who raped her. She wasn't lying about that."

Her explanation placates me only a little. "So if she made a complaint to the police, why did he carry on stalking her? If it was all out in the open, he had to know that even if he wasn't arrested that the police would be watching his every move."

"Like I said, the police didn't believe her. We don't know why for sure. It might have been the past incident. Or there might have been more to it."

I wonder if she's going to make me dig for every detail.

She is.

"Like?" I ask.

"He had friends in the sheriff's office. Some people who made evidence disappear."

"But why didn't he just leave her alone?"

She grips my hand tighter. Almost hurting tight. "Because she had something he wanted."

"What?" I ask, trying to get her to release me. "What did he want?"

Aunt Ginger keeps her eyes fastened to mine as she tries to read me like a book. I give her nothing. Her eyes glisten with tears.

"You," she finally says. "He said he wanted *you*."

Chapter Eight

Cash: $34.50 (I found a ten on the dresser).
Food: OK, if you like homestyle, which I do.
Shelter: Our aunt's house for now.
Weapons: Gun, scissors, ice pick.
Plan: The same. Find Mom. Kill Dad.

THERE IS NO AIR IN the room. Not a single molecule of oxygen. I let out a gasp and Aunt Ginger is all over me. I don't need CPR and I push her away. While I understand what she said, I still feel like the room is spinning and I'm unable to grab ahold of its meaning.

He wanted you.

"Honey," Aunt Ginger says. "Honey, are you all right? Put your head between your knees."

Of course I'm not all right. And I'm not putting my head between my knees. I'm beginning to wonder if Mom ran away from Aunt Ginger that first time because she was bossy and annoying and caring at the same time.

"I'm fine," I finally say as Aunt Ginger makes a move toward the kitchen. She is a streak of long hair and she leaves a trail of concern as she hurries back with some water.

"Drink this," she says. "You're upset. You're dehydrated."

I want to say that everything she said is true. I also want to say that in the past twenty-four hours I've lost my mom, pulled a knife from my dead stepfather's chest, found out that my bio dad was a serial killer, and not only did he want my mom, he wants me. Add Idaho to the list and just about anyone could see that I had ample reason to feel the way I did. Upset didn't cover it.

"Thanks," I say. "It's just hard to take in all of this."

"I know, honey. I can only imagine."

I have calmed down now. I don't know this woman, this sister of my mom, the aunt that I never knew I had, but I do know right then that she only means well. I see the lines around her eyes, the circles that underscore the anxiety that has held her captive since her sister disappeared.

"What do you mean he wanted me?"

"He found out that your mom had gotten pregnant," she says, looking deeply into my eyes. "He made it known that he felt that you belonged to him."

I feel a rush of bile. I could never belong to that rapist. I belonged to the dad who raised me. The dad that my creep of a bio father has murdered. I can't speak for a moment, and looking down I see my hands shake a little.

My silence makes Aunt Ginger uncomfortable. She looks down to one of those old-time braided rugs that has probably been there since the day she and her husband—whoever he was—moved there.

"Rylee. I was there when he came for her . . . and for you."

THE HOSPITAL MATERNITY WARD HAD the shiniest floors Ginger could imagine. A mirror finish, she thought. Their mother was too embarrassed about her daughter's condition to be there for her, so Ginger volunteered to be Courtney's birthing coach. Although she was still sixteen when she delivered, Courtney seemed to be a trooper about the whole thing. After an agonizing—and a little boring—wait for contractions to quicken, the birthing process went off without much of a hitch. Certainly there was screaming and the kind of facial contortions that suggest an imminent demise, and then a baby girl who'd been conceived in darkness was handed from her aunt to her mother.

Courtney didn't look at the baby right away.

"I'm glad it's a girl," she said.

"I was hoping for that too. Look at her. She's beautiful."

Courtney was scrunched up in the bed as a whirlwind of hospital staff flitted about pulling bloody sheets, clamping this and that, stitching here and there.

"I can't look. If I look, I might see him in her."

Tears leaked from her eyes.

"She doesn't."

"It will make it harder to give her up."

"You don't have to."

"I am afraid."

"I know, honey."

AS THE STORY AUNT GINGER tells plays out, I find out more about my mother and my life; and it illuminates so much of what has been hidden in the orchestrated turmoil of our lives. I remember one time when we were watching an episode of *Teen Mom* on TV and the girl who'd just had a baby was talking about giving it up for adoption.

"I could never do that," I said.

"If it is best for the child," Mom replied, "then it is what's best for you. I know people who have considered doing it because, well, it was the only thing to do that was right."

"Ditching your kid? How could that ever be right? I mean, they shouldn't have got pregnant in the first place."

"You're right, but sometimes mistakes happen. Sometimes pregnancies are anything but planned."

I knew Mom had me young. She told me she was eighteen, but now I know she was sixteen. I thought she'd been married to my father, the war hero, but that was a lie too.

"I know people who have made the decision to keep their babies and have regretted it," she had said. "I know others who contemplated the same thing and they now hate themselves for ever having thought so."

I wonder now where I fell on the spectrum my mother had laid bare. Had she regretted keeping me? Had I been the mistake that ruined her life?

AUNT GINGER FIDDLES WITH THE fringe of a burnt-orange colored afghan and continues her story. I pull myself from the memory of my mysterious mother and listen. I am calm now. Riveted really. I know that Aunt Ginger is in the middle of a set of memories charged with emotion and fear. It shows plainly on her face, in the quick movements of her fidgety fingers. I wonder how many times she's told this story. I suspect not many. I suspect no one but her, my mother and my biological father know the truth about how I started life.

"SHE LOOKS LIKE YOU, COURTNEY. She looks like you!"

Courtney removed a cool compress from her brow and looked down as her sister placed her baby next to her. Her breasts had nearly tumbled out of the sheet, and though she was modest, she didn't care. Her eyes were transfixed by the slightly pinched, pink face of the creature that had just emerged from her tattered womb in one slippery final push.

"Hello, little girl," she said.

"She's your baby. Not his," Ginger whispered next to her.

But a nurse caught the remark and shook her head.

"None of my business," she said, "but sometimes it's good to have a man around. At least for child support, if nothing else."

Ginger almost sneered at the nurse. "That'll never happen. Not with this man."

"Just trying to be helpful. None of my business."

"You're right. None."

Courtney wasn't paying attention to the conversation between her sister and the nurse. She was off somewhere else. She was holding her baby, looking down into the unfocused eyes that now latched on to hers with tentative uncertainty.

"I love you, baby of mine," she said. "I'll never let you go. I'll never let anyone hurt you. Never."

AUNT GINGER STOPS HER STORY. She's folded the afghan and she's stiffening her body in a way that indicates she's about to get up. Like the story is over. But it isn't. It didn't get to the part that I want to know about. I don't want, don't need, to know that she almost gave me up. I need to know how it was that my biological father, this Alex Rader, staked a claim for me.

"You can't stop now," I say, too forcefully, and I see her bristle slightly. I try to backpedal to soften my words. "That didn't come out right, Aunt Ginger. What I meant to say, is I really need to know and you're the only one who can tell me. I've spent my life with Mom—alone at first, then with Dad, and then Hayden—but now only Hayden remains. I need to know everything. I need to find my mom."

My words are like grenades to Aunt Ginger's heart. I feel bad about that but what can I do? I don't know her at all. I don't know if she's a liar like my mom. I sense that she's holding back because she cares about me.

"Look," she finally says, blinking back my words. "It happened at the hospital. A security guard, a policeman, I'm not really sure who or what he was. He told your mom. I was there."

"What did he tell her?" I ask.

She starts talking.

THE LAST VISITORS HAD LEFT for the night. They weren't there for Courtney, but for a Mexican woman named Celina who'd had a son the previous afternoon. In marked contrast to Courtney, who had not had a single visitor outside of Ginger, Celina had a steady stream of well-wishers. All were boisterous, joyful. All came with gifts, flowers, and the best intentions for the newest member of her family.

Courtney had not a single tulip on her side of the room.

As Ginger stood to leave, she bent down and kissed her sister. "We'll get through this," she said.

92

"I know . . . for her." Courtney indicated the still-unnamed baby in a clear Lucite incubator next to Courtney's bed.

The door pushed open and a man in a dark blue and gray uniform poked his head into the room. In his arms, a bouquet of red roses, sixteen in all.

"Special delivery," he said without a smile.

"Ms. Morales is sleeping," Ginger answered.

The guy was handsome and he was wearing a uniform. Ginger brushed back her shoulder-length hair and approached him.

"They're for Courtney." He looked over at her.

"From Mom and Dad?" she said hopefully.

With all the tubes attached to her and the raised side rails of the hospital bed, Courtney couldn't really accept the bouquet. Ginger, who wanted to make an impression, reached for them.

"They're stunning," she said.

The officer nodded and then turned to leave.

"Thank you, officer—?" Ginger says, angling for his name. She was trying anything that would get her noticed. She was young, pretty, but single. And, she could never, ever admit it, but there was something about that uniform that melted her like a scoop of vanilla gelato on an August blacktop.

She set the flowers on a tray and handed the card to her sister.

Courtney teared up, maybe a little because of her parents finally accepting her, but mostly because her hormones had joined forces to take over her body, and everything seemed emotional.

She opened the card and her face turned ashen. Her eyes wide. Her hand moved to the incubator unit.

"We need to get the hell out of here," she whispered, her voice raspy, afraid.

"What?" said Ginger. "We can't leave. You just had a baby."

"We need to go now. Right now. Not five minutes from now."

Courtney swung her legs over the edge of the bed. She tore out the tubes in her arms and she let out a soft cry. Not because it hurt like hell, but because in that moment Courtney knew that calling attention to herself was akin to a flashing billboard that said:

Take me. Come and get me. I'm right here.

She pressed the card into Ginger's hands and then she put on her maternity jeans and a top.

"We have to get out of here," she repeated.

Ginger tried to stop her. "You can't," she said. "You just had a baby. You've lost blood. You're not well enough."

Courtney stared at her sister. "He can't have her."

"Who can't, Courtney?"

By then, Courtney had moved to the other side of the room. Her eyes caught those of Ms. Morales, but the woman closed hers without saying anything.

Ginger was beside herself. Her sister had gone insane and she was confused. She wondered if she should call the doctors or the nurses. Her eyes fell on the call button next to the bed.

"Don't," Courtney pleaded.

Ginger looked at the little card. It was the kind that came from the florist. This one didn't come from the florist. A police officer brought it in.

CONGRATULATIONS TO US. BOUND FOREVER. SHE'S MINE. ALWAYS WILL BE. IN TIME, I'LL COME FOR HER.

AS I SIT HERE, GINGER does what I need her to do. She tells

94

me everything. She tells me how my mom and she were certain that the man who had brought the flowers was connected with my mom's rapist. Her tormenter. My father. They decided that he'd been connected to law enforcement and that he'd abducted other girls and that my mom's cleverness had saved her, but then she had me.

"Once you were here," Aunt Ginger says, "there was no way she was going to lose you. She was not going to give you to him."

"She almost gave me away," I say.

She shakes her head. "She never even filled out the paperwork. She never was going to let you go. I think she needed to process what had happened to her before she could do what she was meant to do."

"What was that?" I ask as Aunt Ginger flips off a light and leads me toward the staircase.

"Love you," she says. "Protect you. Be your mom." I know my new aunt is trying to be kind right now, but I'm still so mad at Mom.

Protect me? She betrayed me. She lied to me.

I LIE MOTIONLESS. THE MOON leaves a trail of light across the big old bed that commands almost all of the guest room. I know by looking around that it was a girl's room, but I don't even know her name. I feel bad about that. I haven't asked Aunt Ginger anything about her life. About her estranged children. About her husband. I don't even know if my uncle is dead or alive. It is very late.

Almost two a.m. I hear Aunt Ginger flush the toilet and go back to bed. Ten more minutes pass and I throw off the covers and slide my feet very quietly to the floor. I am already dressed.

After talking with my aunt, I spent hours poring over the letters, the news clippings—the breadcrumbs Mom left for me. Now I grab my things, including my shoes, and tiptoe down the hallway. I've written a note to both my aunt and my brother. But even though I've said everything I need to say, I can't just leave Hayden without saying goodbye.

Or without promising I will be back for him.

Hayden's sleeping nearly at the foot of the bed when I enter his room. His arm dangles to the floor and he looks like a gangly baby lost in slumber. His dyed hair suits him, I think. I lean over his body and he stirs awake.

"Rylee?" he says drowsily, his brow knitted like one of those doilies downstairs. "I wanna sleep now. What's the matter?"

God, I love him.

"I'm going to find Mom."

"I'll come, too," he says, with the kind of conviction used by a girl telling another she looks cute in the worst outfit in the world.

"No. You can't," I say. "I promise I'll be back."

My brother opens, then closes his eyes and I do something that I haven't done in a long, long time. I kiss Hayden on the forehead. "Love you," I say.

"I'll take care of him," a voice behind me says in a whisper.

I turn around and find my aunt in the doorway. She's wearing a pretty grape-colored robe and she's holding a bag and a set of car keys.

"You drive, don't you?" she asks.

"Of course I do," I say.

Chapter Nine

Cash: $234.50 (Aunt Ginger gave me ten twenties).
Food: A box of granola bars too.
Shelter: Ford Focus.
Weapons: Gun, scissors, ice pick.
Plan: Try not to get picked up by the police. Find Mom. Then kill Dad.

THE FORD FOCUS IS A CAR for losers, but I'm hoping that luck is on my side. It's a mega hope. The truth is that I'm not a seasoned driver. Far, far from it. I've never passed my test. I *did* get behind the wheel a few times to move a car into the driveway, and Caleb liked Grand Theft Auto and to sync up better with him, I played that game about a zillion times. *Alone.* Without him. Just to be close to him. When I remember that right now, I think maybe I am a loser after all. Maybe the Ford Focus my aunt is letting me use is an appropriate car.

The car is a conspicuous red. Aunt Ginger has—or rather had—a plastic potato hanging from the rear-view mirror. On the front of the plastic potato is the tag-line *Idaho's Spuds Number One in the World.* All I could think about when I pitched the thing into the backseat was that it must be really rough being from a state in which your marquee item is a lowly brown tuber.

Right now I want French fries. I don't know why.

In that instant, I catch myself in the mirror. It startles me a little how much I look like my mother. With the dye job, the heavier, mom-ish make-up, and the not-so-bad-if-I-say-so-myself haircut, I really *could* pass for her. That's a good thing. If I get pulled over I have her driver's license.

I am Candace.

As I drive west on the Interstate, I munch on a granola bar and think about where I'm going and what I need to do. At first, it's scary driving so fast and my hands hold the steering wheel with a deathly grip. My knuckles literally hurt. But as I keep going, I grow more confident, but I'm also tired. It is early morning and I pull over and sleep a little at a rest stop next to a minivan with steamed up windows. A little girl opens her eyes and I nod at her. I wonder for a second if she's on the run too. I'd been that little girl in the past, sleeping in our car, waiting. I don't remember exactly where that was or how old I was. Her age? Five?

I remember my mom talking to a woman at the rest area and how she'd offered us money because she saw something in us that I didn't understand.

Homelessness.

Like that minivan and that little girl.

The vehicle is loaded to the gills with stuff. I look closer and recognize that they aren't camping. They aren't moving. They are living there. It's just the man behind the wheel and the little girl. Where is her mother?

A trail from the van leads to the restroom.

I call the girl Selma for some reason. She's pretty. She has dark hair and dark eyes. I catch her eyes again. Selma moves her finger through the condensation on the window that she stares out from. A circle. Two dots. Finally, an arch.

A sad face.

She'll be better off than I am.

I can't help her.

I don't even know if she needs help, though deep down I sense that she does. The swarthy man looks from the driver's side and gives me a scowl and I turn away, slipping down deeper in my seat. I check the door locks. Down.

The visit to Aunt Ginger plays in my head like the DVR when my mom pushes past all the commercials. I think of the papers from the safe deposit box and what they mean. One now makes sense—the card from the hospital—it wasn't someone wishing happiness for a new mother, but someone making a claim on her.

And on me.

A birth certificate confounds me. There is no name. Or at least, if there was one it has been carefully removed. I can understand why she didn't want *his* name on the document that announced my existence on this planet, but why no name in the space provided for one?

I start driving and by the outskirts of Spokane I even turn on the radio. I can't find anything good to listen to, so I push the button for the CD. Aunt Ginger, it seems, is a country and western fan and, outside of Taylor Swift, I'm not so much into that scene. The song is about drinking and riding in a truck and it is catchy enough to keep it on. I don't love it. Yet I'm alone and the man's voice seems a little bit like company.

I figure that the best course is to start at the beginning. I need to know more about what happened to Megan, Leanne, Shannon, and my mom, to try to make a plan to find my bio dad. Since Mom is missing and the three girls are dead, that doesn't leave me with tons of options.

When I finally make it over the mountain pass to North Bend, Washington, I stop at a Starbucks drive-through because I need some coffee—and I've never driven through any drive-through and I want to see if my wobbly driving skills have improved since Idaho. I don't clip the order window, but I come close. I order a sandwich and a latte and I realize that I can never do that again. When you don't have a home, and you don't have any source of income, eight dollars is too much for anything as frivolous as coffee and a sandwich. I ask the girl with mocha-colored hair and eyes, a requirement for working there, I guess, where the library is located.

"Turn right out of the lot. Take the next left. Go to the light. Then take another left and you're right there."

Right. Left. Light. Left. And was that last "right" a direction or an affirmation that I'd be at the library?

I pull over in the parking lot and inhale the sandwich. I barely chew it. I didn't realize I was so hungry. Or nervous. Or that turkey and pesto is a bad combination. If I'm scarfing it down because I'm nervous, well, I'm nervous about that too. I don't want to end up being an emotional eater like Marilee at school. The girl eats three lunches every day and pukes most of it up. I've been in the bathroom when she's done the puking part and it is probably the ugliest sound in the world.

Scratch that. *Second ugliest.* The ugliest sound in the world was the one made when I pulled the hunting knife from my dad's chest.

The library is either new or recently remodeled. Bright colored carpet tiles mark the children's reading space; more muted colors indicate adult areas. I stop at the periodical section and skim through the morning papers to see if there's an update on what happened in Port Orchard. But there isn't. I don't know what to make of that. Dad was killed. Mom, Hayden and I are missing. Surely that deserves some more follow up. Maybe later. As far as the Seattle paper goes, Port Orchard is the other side of the moon anyway. I go to an area with a bunch of computers and a sign saying COOL TEEN SCENE—obviously named by some adult who didn't understand that calling something "cool" makes it completely so not.

As I drop my purse to the floor and position myself in front of a computer, I am promptly told by some kid that I'm too old to be there.

"This is for teens," he says, pointing up at the sign on the wall. He smells like he went swimming in body spray. "Not adults."

I stare hard at him. I know my mom's hair and style make me look older, but come on, there's no way I look like an adult. I'm fifteen. Or sixteen. Somewhere around there, anyway.

"How would you like me to punch you in the gut? I'll do it so fast and so quietly no one will hear. And if you say anything, I'll say you groped my tits."

His hooded lids snap open. "You're kidding?"

I stare harder. I don't say the words, but one begins with an F; the other with an O.

He backs off and leaves. A trail of Axe follows him like snail slime.

I'm not sure where that little bit of rage came from, but I suspect my bio father's side of the family. My knuckles are white. I'm stressed out about what I'll find when I cross the mountains. I know my mom and creep of a father are here somewhere. All his victims are. Alex Rader, if that's his name, wouldn't stray far from the best moments of his insufferable, twisted life.

Creeps like him always love to bask in the memory of what they've done. I've watched enough TV to know that.

I log on to the computer with a keyboard that looks like someone jammed a cookie into it and start searching. I read more and more about Shannon, Megan, and Leanne. There are no articles about my mom. Not a single one. After talking to Aunt Ginger, I know why.

No one believed her. Her own parents didn't. There was no one to stand up for her to say they were worried she was missing. Even her own sister. I wonder why *she* didn't. She seemed to love her.

I search for Alex Rader, but that's an epic fail. There are several of the unfortunately named men in the country, but none locally. I don't allow myself to think that the man I'm looking for would simply move away and start over. I'm thinking that Alex Rader wasn't a real name. Maybe he changed his name all the time?

Just like we did.

I scan for more clippings about Shannon Blume's case. She

was last seen two blocks from her home in Burien, Washington. I see the same article that Mom had clipped and put in the safe deposit box. There are others too. I take in the information faster than I did that expensive Starbucks sandwich. I also hit the copy feature and I hear the whirring of the laser printer behind me.

There's a picture of Shannon. A school photo, I think. She looks somewhat blankly at the camera. Her hair is blond, long and parted in the middle. All the girls were blond. Her photo is shown in what appears to be a wooden frame, held by her mother. Her father has his arm around her. Their eyes are not blank at all. Mr. and Mrs. Blume's eyes telegraph their fear. Fear that would be well founded.

Ten days later another article appears.

TRANSIENT FINDS BODY OF MISSING BURIEN TEEN

A subsequent report indicates that the girl had been bound and gagged. The reporter uses the word "violated".

Raped too, I think, but the paper doesn't say so.

And finally, as I speed-read and print, I see the end of Shannon's story. The transient was arrested and convicted of her murder.

There are three articles about the trial. I skim these too. The jury was convinced, but Mom wasn't. I reach for the fake Chanel purse and pull out the envelope with the clipping. Mom has underlined a sentence.

Blume had recently had a heart tattooed on her shoulder, although her mother had no knowledge of it.

103

My mother thought that was significant and I need to know why.

I search for the Blumes' address and find through online tax records that they haven't moved.

The smelly body-spray kid glowers at me from across the room, trying to get me to leave. I glance over at the computer next to me—the one he'd been using. Two under-dressed women and what appears to be a German Shepherd are doing something on the screen that I don't even want to process. Along with being degrading and humiliating, it is completely at odds with the stated purpose of the "Cool Teen Scene".

EXPLORE YOUR WORLD. IT'S A BIG, BEAUTIFUL PLACE!

I look at him and mouth the word: "*Perv!*"

I don't even wait for his reaction. I have too much to do. Next I look up information about victim number two. She's another pretty blonde. And she's sixteen at the time of her disappearance. Megan Moriarty was on the cheerleading squad at Kentridge High School in a suburb further south of Seattle. I look at her and make a judgement. I don't think I would have liked her. I know that it's wrong. But for some reason I never like the girls on the cheerleading squad. They are so over-the-top in their self-indulgence that if you weren't a mirror they'd never look at you. At least they never looked at me. Caleb Hunter said I was way prettier than the six girls that considered South Kitsap their personal turf and the rest of us either servants (band members, coaches) or adoring fans (the suck-ups that make up most of the class). Outsiders like me hated them, but we were also kind of mesmerized by them too. Every second of the day the gang of six demonstrated their power. They were interchangeable—slender, larger on top, and teeth as white as ascending wedding doves. They could snare a boy with just a look.

I think of Caleb just now. I had told myself that I'd never see him again. When I did that, I just assumed that I could will him out of my memory. We'd done that as a family before, when we made the switch. We just packed up whatever we had that we needed and left everything else and everyone else behind. We didn't disappear in the night. We couldn't do that. That, Mom said, would arouse suspicion. Instead, we told neighbors and casual friends—because that's all we ever had—that a family emergency had occurred and we had to leave. We promised to call and write, but we never did. Not even once.

I miss him.

I'm over him.

We never were anything anyway.

I try and shut him out, but instead I find myself logging on to Facebook.

I HAVE TOLD MYSELF OVER and over not to do what I'm about to do, but I can't help it. The familiar blue of the Facebook login looks at me from the screen and dares me. I type in my email address and my password. I stupidly accepted some of the kids at South Kitsap as "friends"—only because I'd been goaded into it.

By Caradee Hagen of all people.

I remember the moment when she studied me like a lab experiment as we stood by her locker. She was fiddling with her smartphone.

I should have known better as she scrolled to my minuscule Facebook page.

"Rylee, it looks like someone is a bit of a loner."

Her words so dripped with fake concern that I almost wanted to pull her aside and give her lessons on how to act sincere.

But I didn't.

Instead, I lied.

"I had a stalker at my last school and had to start over," I said.

She shot me a look of admiration. One that should be fake, but was genuine.

"Holy crap," she said, a little too gleefully. "That's so cool."

"I guess," I answered, knowing that Caradee is a complete attention skank and she'd no doubt welcome a stalker. Sure, she'd act all mad and scared, but deep down she'd love being in the center of such a drama.

"I'll friend you right now," she said, pushing the request button on her phone and waiting for me to accept. I didn't want to, but I logged in and accepted.

"Let's take a selfie right now and I'll post it," she said, holding up her phone and getting into position.

And, of course, since Caradee is in control, the photo she posted is great of her. My eyes are halfway shut and the angle makes me look about ten pounds heavier.

And that's just my face.

I really don't like that girl.

And now, here I am, on Facebook, looking to see if the only friend I really ever had is online. Immediately, my pulse quickens.

The little green light next to his name is on.

My fingers tremble a little and I don't exactly know why. I take them from the keyboard and give them a shake, as though whatever was causing the tremor was physical and not emotional. I will not crack. But I will not let Caleb Hunter think that leaving town as my brother and I did was something that was easy to do.

His picture makes me smile. He's got his arms folded in some kind of tough guy pose and a sheepish grin on his face. I took that photo. Two days ago at school. Forty-eight hours before my world spun out of control.

Before the knife.

The blood.

The truth about where I came from.

And the mystery of where Mom has been taken.

I put my hands back on the keyboard and type two words.

I'M SORRY.

I wait. Nothing. Maybe he's away from the computer. Maybe Facebook is acting up again. Maybe he's blocked me. I type some more.

ARE YOU THERE?

Another moment passes and my heart sinks so low into my abdomen, I'm sure that I will need surgery to put it back where it belongs.

And then, like a blast of air through the room, words are thrown at me.

RYLEE! WHAT HAPPENED? WHERE ARE YOU?

I won't need that surgery after all.

I CAN'T SAY.

He answers right away.

YOU DIDN'T OFF YOUR OLD MAN?

That he would even ask it makes me wonder how well I know him. Or how well I think I do. And yet I don't blame him. Not really. He has a reason to ask. I would probably ask too.

I type: *YOU KNOW BETTER.*

Again, he responds without a beat to waste.

WHERE THE HELL ARE YOU?

I don't want to lie to him. So I shut him down. At least, I give it my best shot.

DON'T ASK. IT'S COMPLICATED.

It doesn't work. Not completely anyway. He answers right back.

WHAT'S COMPLICATED IS HOW YOU JUST DISAPPEARED ON ME. WTF! YOU'RE ALL OVER THE NEWS. I THOUGHT YOU WERE DEAD OR SOMETHING.

He cares. I get that.

I look around and suck in some air. Since I'm uncertain about what to say, I type the obvious.

I'M NOT DEAD.

THANKS FOR LETTING ME KNOW. I'VE BEEN SCARED SHITLESS.

His response is so Caleb. He's angry, sarcastic. But he cares and I know it. Given all that I've been through in the hours since my dad's murder, that's all I need right now.

I type a response and my fingertip hovers a little before I send.

I JUST WANTED YOU TO KNOW THAT YOU MATTER TO ME.

Caleb Hunter must have taken Advanced Keyboarding in his freshman year because his response is instantaneous.

I KNOW THAT. WHAT HAPPENED?

I drink in more air and type.

I CAN'T GET INTO IT. LIKE I SAID IT'S COMPLICATED.

He drops a tiny bomb at me.

THANKS FOR TRUSTING ME.

My heart sinks again. *Ugh*. And my hands tremble a little more. Suddenly the screen seems fuzzy and I strain to see the chat window as I put the words into order and hit the SEND button.

IT ISN'T ABOUT TRUSTING YOU.

Part of me wants to say more, but I know that I can't yet. All I ever wanted was to be normal or something close to normal. Caleb made me feel that was all possible. He could be trusted. Liars like me know how to spot another phony better than anyone. Mom said more than once "it takes one to know one" when she sized up those we met when we were on the run.

The people who were hiding, running, trying to blend in without being noticed—Mom insisted she could smell the fear on the people like us.

I blink hard and the screen clears, but only for a flash.

I CAN HELP. I WANT TO HELP. YOU DON'T HAVE TO DO WHATEVER YOU ARE DOING ALONE, RYLEE.

I know Caleb means it. But I also know that what I'm about to do, I need to do alone. I can't involve another person that I care about, even though all I want to do is go to him and tell him that he means more to me than anyone.

Except my little brother. My mother. My dead stepfather.

And the man I'm going to find and kill.

I type what I hope are not the last words that I'll ever direct toward him.

I HAVE TO GO.

I think about adding something about my feelings, but I'm not good at that. I don't know how to say what I'm feeling and, really, I don't want the distraction of those feelings. Not now.

Probably not ever.

I look sideways at the screen, as though facing it head on would hurt more.

DON'T SHUT ME OUT.

I turn away from his message on the screen. I can't answer. I leave those words to twist in the vast void of internet.

I REFOCUS ON WHY I'M HERE. The clock is ticking. I read how Megan had been dropped off by her best friend in front of the Kmart where she worked—a fact that made me like her a little bit. I mean, Kmart. That had to be a come-down for a cheerleader. No wonder her friend dropped her off.

And she was never seen again.

Alive, that is.

A headline wraps around my neck like a strangler's hands:

MISSING CHEERLEADER FOUND IN DUMPSTER

No one deserves that. Not even a cheerleader. I scan the article for the salient points. Missing twelve days. Found battered and partially decomposed in a dumpster behind the Kmart where she worked. Her boyfriend, Kim Mock, found guilty of her murder and imprisoned for life.

I search the local directories and find out that her mom has moved. Her dad might still be at the address in the paper, but

I'm not taking any chances. I print out the articles and the directions to both.

The third girl was Leanne Delmont, also sixteen. According to the news articles, Leanne had been missing for more than three weeks when her body was found, east of Seattle. The case went unsolved until the arrest and a deluge of confessions made by a notorious deal-seeking serial killer named Arnold Cantu. His admittance of guilt meant that he was spared the death penalty. It seems Mr. Cantu was afraid of being on the receiving end of something so barbaric—and deserving—as the gallows, the method of capital punishment reserved for the worst offenders in Washington.

I recall that same article among the papers from the bank. Mom had made a notation. I fish it out of the envelope:

She was one too. I saw her.

Saw her? Saw her when? Where? I don't understand.

In any case, I capture Leanne's family's local address. I wonder what connection Arnold Cantu had with the case. *If any.* Mom seemed emphatic in the way she scrawled that note with a heavy hand, next to Leanne's name.

I saw her.

I gather up all the printouts, more pages than I could manage to read at the moment. I have to get moving. I need to get closer to where he did his hunting, his capturing and his killing. I have to find out everything I can. My time is measured. And it's running out.

"Did you pay for your copies?" the annoying pervy kid says. "Ten cents a page."

"Do you pay to look at pornography?" I ask. My eyes steady

at him, unflinching.

I don't understand where this new, aggressive me is coming from. It scares me a little when my mind races to the changes in my behavior. It isn't like me to confront anyone. I was always the person in the background trying to fit in, trying to be a part of something without really being a part of it. It was like I was the puzzle piece from the wrong box. I could be made to fit in, but not so neatly.

"You think you're real smart, don't you?" he says. "Real tough."

I keep my expression completely flat. "You don't even know."

He seems undeterred. "Well maybe I want to know," he says.

Wrong response. Right there behind the *new books* rack I kick him in the nuts so hard that he can't yell out.

"Do not mess with me, perv," I say.

He slumps to the floor. In my past life I'd tell Mom about my attempts to try on a new persona whenever we moved. I've never tried this one before. I've never been the tough-talking bitch.

Seems I am now. And I kind of like it.

ON MY WAY TO THE front door I glance over at the gasping kid and linger like I'm not afraid that he'll tell on me by looking at the community bulletin board. That's the place where people try to sell things, give away stuff nobody really wants, and promote local events that promise to fill an afternoon with fun, but seldom do. Sometimes I see flyers with missing kids' pictures there, but not today.

Not mine or Hayden's. At least not yet.

An idea comes to me. Somehow in the nightmare that my

life has become, I manage a smile. I take a *lost cat* poster from the board. Seconds later, I turn the key on the ignition and pull out into the trickle of traffic.

I STOP IN AT THE local newspaper. I'd seen the sign on the drive in to the library. I remember almost everything. That's one thing I know I'm good at. The *North Bend Courier* is in a nondescript strip mall. It smells of pizza—the restaurant next door has a powerful kitchen exhaust system.

"Is it free to put in a classified ad for a found cat?" I ask, my face melting into a look of worry, hope, and concern.

A girl looks up from a desk by the front door. She is in her twenties with a halo of black hair that I admire for its sheer mass, if nothing else. She sits in a cubicle by the door and if the space were any smaller I think she'd have to cut her hair. Or I could. I didn't do that bad of a job of my own on that ferry boat ride.

"Yeah," she says. "Tracy can help you."

I go over to a desk in a deadly quiet newsroom. Tracy is her early twenties too. Her hair is long, black, and flows like a silky curtain. Her nameplate says she's the assistant editor, but when I look around, I think that she's probably the boss of the whole sad little office.

"I'll take the info," she says in a clipped and excited voice. I wonder what she'd be like on the scene of a homicide if she's this thrilled about a found cat.

I give her bogus contact information, including Leanne's name and a phone number culled from a boy offering home clean-up services. Then I provide the specifics of this phantom cat and for some reason I lay it on thick. Her unbridled

113

appreciation for what I'm doing for the cat kind of makes me head in to the realm of over-the-top.

"I don't know," I say. "I kind of want to keep her. But my boyfriend's allergic."

"So unlucky," she says.

"He's kind of a creep lately. I actually caught him looking at disgusting porn. I'll probably dump him, but the landlord says I can't have a cat anyway."

"That's so wrong. Pets are people too."

I wasn't sure if she really said that or if I'm going crazy.

"Can you describe her?"

I nod wistfully.

"She's kind of creamy and orange. Like a big orange sherbet float. I know I shouldn't name her, but I've been calling her PC for Peaches and Cream."

"That's so sweet!"

"She's cute. Cuddly and cute." I've got what I wanted so I wrap it up. "I know someone is probably crying their eyes out right now."

"We'll find her family," she says, her almond eyes telegraphing complete certainty.

If I actually had a lost cat, I'd take my information to Tracy, for sure.

A moment later, I'm out the door. My name, at least on my business card, is Tracy Lee. I'm not Asian. But Lee could be any kind of name. It'll work for what I need it to do.

Chapter Ten

Cash: $226.50.
Food: Three granola bars.
Shelter: Car.
Weapons: Gun, scissors, ice pick.
Plan: Find out what happened to Leanne, Shannon and Megan.

THE HOUSE LOOKS JUST AS it did when it appeared in the papers online. It is a single-story rambler with white shutters and matching window boxes, though they are empty now. In front stands a monkey-puzzle tree that has grown nearly as tall as the roofline. That's the only difference that I can really discern as I get out of my car. It is almost lunchtime and the sandwich made me sick. I had to stop at a McDonald's in Burien to use the bathroom. It might have been the turkey and pesto. But it's more likely nerves. Judging by their photo in the paper, Don and Debra Blume would be in their mid-sixties by now, which I hope means they are retired and at home. My hope is confirmed when I peer through the window of the garage and see two cars. One, surprisingly, is a Ford Focus. I'll act as though I love my car or hate it. Depending on whatever they say about theirs. If that comes up. You know, while we're chatting about their dead daughter.

Mrs. Blume answers the door with a wary but kind smile.

I tell her I'm with the *North Bend Courier*.

"You probably heard about our series on Marilee Watson? She was murdered last year. My publisher wanted me to do a new series about how people cope after a tragedy. Can I talk to you and Mr. Blume?"

"You *can't* cope after a tragedy, miss . . . ?" she searches for my name. A pause hangs in the air.

"Tracy Lee." I hand her my business card.

"That's kind of the point of my article," I say. "My Aunt Ginger was killed in a car wreck and I know it's not the same as what happened to Shannon, but my mom has never gotten over it either. I'm including my thoughts about that in the article too. But it can't be about me."

She studies me with flinty eyes. I wonder if she's reminded of her daughter. If she thinks I'm too young for the job. If she's just having a bad day. Maybe every day after you lose a child to murder is a bad day.

"It was a long time ago," she says, her eyes still on mine. "We really don't like reliving it. I'm sure you can understand that."

Of course I can. I hate that I'm opening some old, never-really-healed wounds, but I have no choice.

"Look, it isn't my intent to hurt you again. I'm looking for understanding. I'm trying to tell a story that will bring awareness to community," I say, my brain on overdrive trying to find a way to a yes. I'm not lying to Mrs. Blume. All of those things are true. Except the part about the article that I'm writing.

116

And the part about the real reason why I'm there.

Mrs. Blume takes a step back.

"Please," I say, "I think it is really important that people learn the truth."

Mrs. Blume reaches for the door handle, but hesitates.

"What truth?" she asks.

This is my opening. This is the only moment that I'll have with her if I can't win her over.

"That some hurts never go away," I answer. "That others who have gone through what you have experienced aren't alone and they don't need to feel bad about the lingering pain."

She nods. "All right, Tracy."

I've won her over. I feel tremendous relief, but also a little sick for lying to someone about something so tragic, so important.

"I would have called," I say, pulling myself together, "but with cellphones these days no one has a landline anymore."

She waves me inside. The house is neat, clean, and frozen in time. The furnishings, the decor—even the air feels like it is old. The foyer is devoid of anything personal. A Boston Fern the size of a Mini Cooper fills most of the space.

Someone has a green thumb.

"I was making a frozen pizza," she says, eyeing me with what are now very kind eyes. "Want to stay for lunch?"

Someone wants to barf.

"I'm starving," I quickly say. "I haven't eaten all day. Thank you." I've been there two minutes and I've already lied to this nice woman five or six times. I have no choice, of course. If I told her the truth she'd probably laugh at me and call the police. That would ruin my plans and kill my mother.

Debra Blume is a beautiful woman. I can see, however, how the years and the loss of her daughter reveal the undying agony around her eyes. They are blue, but a weary shade of blue. The color of a pair of jeans that I once loved so much, but ruined when I stupidly put too much bleach in the washer. I wanted to speed up the fading process. Instead, I annihilated the hue.

Donald Blume comes out. He's older than she is, but he has a nice smile and I like him right away.

"Doing a story about our little girl?" he says, sinking in to what I assume is "his" chair, a big old leather club chair.

I nod, but answer in the negative. "Not really. I mean, about her, but about how her loss impacted, you know, on you and your family."

"It'll be a short story," he says.

Mrs. Blume disappears into the kitchen.

"How is that?" I ask. For the first time I spot Shannon's shrine. There are nearly a dozen pictures of a girl my age lining the mantle and a large silver urn, which I can only assume holds her remains. I don't know why people keep ashes. I don't get that at all. The person was not the residue of their burned up flesh and pulverized bones. The person was the spirit and that left when she was brutally killed.

By my bio dad.

"It ruined us. Plain and simple. I took to drinking. Debra took to antidepressants until she had to go to treatment."

"I'm sorry."

"Me too," he says. "But . . . " His words trail off and behind his glasses I see the sheen of tears. "But the short story is that it ruined our lives. She was everything."

118

I nod and Mrs. Blume returns with a slice of pizza. I almost hurl. It's chicken and pesto.

"Looks wonderful," I say, thinking of how I'm going to eat that slice. I thought of saying I was gluten-free, but I'm not. It always freaks me out when people announce that, like being gluten-free is a badge of honor. I need these people to like me. I need them to tell me what they know. I need to process all of it and somehow figure out where my mother is being held captive.

As we eat, the Blumes start at the beginning. They talk, they cry, they tell me about the kind of hurt that comes when forced to identify their daughter on a gurney through the thick glass of a morgue's viewing room. They tell me that they regret they didn't tell her they loved her as much as they should have. I watch as Mrs. Blume puts a trembling hand on her husband's. She's the stronger of the two. She knows that whatever regrets she has are smaller than the burden he carries. He asks her to get him a drink.

"And don't be stingy on it, either," he says.

I mutter something about being sorry and it's the first time I'm not really lying to them. I am sorry. I feel sick, and it isn't the pesto chicken pizza either.

"At least you got some justice," I say. "At least the killer was caught and punished."

She looks at me dead in the eyes. "That's what they tell us," she says.

The remark is odd.

She looks at her husband and he shrugs his shoulders as though it is all right for her to speak, though I doubt there was ever a time when he could stop her.

"Honestly, Tracy," she begins, "we never really felt comfortable with the prosecution of Steve Jones, that homeless man, for the murder of our daughter. Don't get me wrong." She stops and catches her husband's gaze. "Don't get *us* wrong. We don't doubt the prosecution did the best they could but, well, we sort of believed Mr. Jones's alibi."

"You did?" I fumble for the words. "I don't remember what it was?"

"He said he'd been out drinking and had a blackout. A friend said he was picked up by the police. The next thing Jones knew was that he was in front of our dead daughter's body. Sirens woke him up."

"Who called it in?" I ask.

Mr. Blume cuts in. "Anonymous did. Whoever *that* was. The police tape was lost before trial. They could talk about what the caller said, but they couldn't provide any evidence that the tape really existed."

"Are you saying you thought he might have been set up?" I ask.

"That's a stretch," Mrs. Blume says as she clears the dishes. I look down and to my surprise, I've eaten the pizza. I'm going to pay for it later, I know. "We think someone tampered with the evidence. I don't know why. Maybe to make sure they'd convict. I guess we should be happy about it—and at the time we were."

"But not now?" I ask.

Mr. Blume answers. "No. We just don't believe they ever answered how she got that tattoo and where she was the

120

week she was gone. They made it sound like she'd been held captive somewhere by Jones—apparently he'd been staying in the basement of a church."

"I don't know about the tattoo, but why don't you think church basement?"

"Because the walls were paper thin. Shannon sang in the school choir. She had a set of lungs on her. She would have made some noise. No one at the Marine Lookout Apartments heard a peep."

"What about the tattoo?" I ask. "I don't get that."

I look down at my printouts, scanning for more details.

"Shannon would never have gotten a tattoo," Mr. Blume says. He gets up and shows me a picture of her, taken at a Highline High School performance of *Les Miserables*. "She played Cosette. She was beautiful and perfect."

"Yes, she was," I say.

"She told me that tattoos degraded the human body. She said God had made everyone beautiful and perfect and that no one had a right to screw up what He had done."

"I don't like tattoos either," I say, though I don't really have an opinion on the subject. I can't get one until I'm eighteen, anyway. And that isn't for two or three years.

Mrs. Blume picks up the family cat and it purrs immediately.

"Gloria was Shannon's cat. She's eighteen."

I'm not sure what to say. That it's nice they still have her? That I bet the cat misses Shannon too? As the cat purrs I change the subject back to the tattoo.

"What was the tattoo that she had? I don't see a mention of its design in the papers."

Mr. Blume clears his throat. "It was a heart with the numerals 16 in the middle of it."

"Where was it on her body?"

"Her right shoulder," he answers, ice tinkling in the glass of soda from which he's been drinking. At least I hope it's soda. I hope both Shannon's parents are on the mend. I don't pray much anymore. I haven't for a long time, but tonight I will for them.

"Why wasn't the tattoo's design in the paper?" I ask.

Mrs. Blume takes this one. "The detective wanted to leave it out. You know, in case it was done by our daughter's killer."

"Which it was," Mr. Blume says, slurring his words a little. Okay, now I'm sure. When Mr. Blume asked his wife not to be stingy with the drink, it had nothing to do with the number of ice cubes she put in it. His head bobs slightly. He is getting drunk.

"What was the detective's name?" I ask.

Mrs. Blume ponders it for a moment and I let her. No need to plant a seed when looking for the truth.

She turns to her husband. "What was his name, Donald?"

His lids are heavy and he looks at her. "Donald is my name," he says.

"Yes, honey," she says, looking sadly at him then over at me with the look of a woman who's been there before. Too many times. She's embarrassed, but resigned to the situation. I feel sorry for her. I'm glad that she still has that bag-of-bones cat. Mrs. Blume looks to me.

"I'm sorry. I'm not good with names. My husband is," she says, "Or at least he used to be."

122

"The name would really help my story," I say, though inside I want to scream at her and tell her that my mom's being held captive somewhere—if she's alive—and I need to find out where. I need help. A lead. Even just a name would be something.

I say none of that, of course, because my mind switches to a new thought, a memory is coming into focus. I'm remembering something else as I watch Shannon's mother put a thin blue blanket over her now sleeping husband. With the reminiscence comes a jolt. It comes at me quick and I'm almost breathless.

I WAS FOUR. MY MOTHER and I were out by the above-ground pool that the previous tenants of our rental house had left behind. I honestly can't remember exactly where it was. There was a huge tree that hung over most of the backyard like a circus canopy. It was so hot that day that Mom actually got into the pool with me. I remember how she played "motorboat" and dragged me from one end of the pool to the other, laughing and making sure that when I laughed I didn't drink in any water. When she grew tired of the game, I begged her to continue. That day, Mom never let me down. No matter what was on her mind, she was always present with me in the moment. When I became tired and hungry, she hoisted me to the edge of the pool and we ate cheese sandwiches and drank apple juice.

I remember how I hugged her and for the very first time noticed the faded lines of a heart on her shoulder.

I said something about it and she got up and carried me inside. It was like my words, my curiosity about that heart, had shut her down. Hurt her.

The next day Mom took me to the emergency room. There was nothing wrong with me, but she'd injured her shoulder.

I don't remember how. Later, when I was older, I asked her about the big scar and she told me that she'd slipped on the shower floor and smashed the glass. When I asked her which house she told me Iowa. I looked at her. I knew when she was lying.

The house in Iowa had a tub with a shower curtain. There had never been a glass shower door.

MRS. BLUME AND I TALK some more. I wasn't sure what I had hoped to find out, but I feel that I have learned something. When she asks me if she should call if she remembers anything else, I shake my head and make a face.

"The number on the card is not going to be any good soon. We're having a new phone system installed. Ugh. You know how all that phone stuff goes."

"I guess so," she says. "It took us forever to sort out our cable bill."

I smile. "I'm staying at the Best Western in Kent tonight."

She looks at me strangely. "You're so close to home."

I shrug a little, as though I'm annoyed. Not at her. But at the reason I now have to invent for why I am staying in a motel instead of driving twenty minutes back to North Bend. Stupid me.

"My sister lives there and I promised her we'd have a girls' night," I say.

"That's nice," she says. "Family's important."

I start for the door. I'm sick about lying to these nice people.

Yet I know that these are small lies compared to the ones that have surrounded me all my life.

"All right then," I say. "Bye." I look over at her husband, asleep in his chair. "Tell Mr. Blume goodbye. I'm so sorry for your loss, Mrs. Blume."

She lingers in the doorway as I get into my car.

All I can think about is my mother and that tattoo on her shoulder and how she had probably cut it out with a knife. Shannon had one too. I wonder if they all had the same tattoo. As I pull away, I come up with a nickname for my piece-of-crap serial killer father.

The Sweet Sixteen Killer.

Creeps like him always get a stupid name.

He doesn't know it yet, of course, but he'll only be known as the Sweet Sixteen Killer *after* I take him out. He'll never get to enjoy his fame the way that I will revel in his death.

Chapter Eleven

Cash: $113.
Food: One granola bar, one slice chicken & pesto pizza.
Shelter: Best Western Motel, Kent, Washington.
Weapons: Gun, scissors, ice pick.
Plan: Find Mom. Take out the Sweet 16 killer.

THE CLERK AT THE FRONT DESK doesn't give me much trouble when she asks for a credit card and I tell her I don't have one. With a pissed off look on my face, I say that I was a victim of identify theft and my credit cards are all messed up. I'm pretty convincing. She takes it in and says the same thing happened to her best friend. The billing policy, she says, is to have a credit card for incidentals, but the truth is that at the Best Western there aren't any incidentals. I fork over $111 and some change for two nights' stay, tell her I'm here for a couple of days to see my sister, Megan, and go to my room on the second floor. The room smells of disinfectant and bleach and I'm guessing that's supposed to reinforce that it's clean. I wonder what they were trying to disinfect that made it in need of so much cleanser.

Since there are two beds, I use one to spread out all of my research materials. I don't have as much as I think I do. The clippings from Mom's safe deposit box, the printouts from the day's stop at the library and a few notes that I made when talking to the Blumes. I scoped out this motel because I knew it was near Megan Moriarty's parents' house. It also faces the Kmart where she was last seen, and where her killer dumped her like she was nothing more than a bundle of expired submarine sandwiches from the discount store's deli.

The other reason I chose the motel—besides its location and the fact I knew it was cheap—was the fact they'd advertised having a business center with a computer work station for the "exclusive use of our guests".

I look at the "courtesy alarm clock" and it's almost five.

I see myself in the mirror and I am reminded again of my mother. I wonder where she is. If she's alive. If he's only holding her until he finds me, though I fully intend to find him first. Then I think of Hayden. He was so sleepy that I know he didn't get the full import of what I was telling him early that morning. The day is more than half over. I want nothing more for him right now than to know that I can do this. I will kill that father freak. I will bring Mom home. We won't have to run anymore. We can be a family.

And then I remember to say that prayer. I haven't prayed in the longest time, but I get on my knees. I promise God that I will do whatever he wants me to do. In exchange, I ask for peace for Shannon's parents. I pray that Mr. Blume will stop drinking. I pray that Mrs. Blume will be able to grieve for her daughter without the complications of covering up for the man she so clearly loves. I pray for Hayden. I pray for my mother and then I head out the door.

THE CAR IS ON "E" and I pull alongside the gas pump only to find out that the gas tank is on the other side. I try to maneuver the car around to the other side without looking like an idiot. The gas station attendant gives me a weird expression, so I'm pretty sure that I do look stupid right then. After filling up, which cuts my cash reserves by another $40, I drive slowly past the Kmart to the Moriartys' house on James Street. Kent feels a lot like Port Orchard. Bigger, to be sure. But just a little sad. I watch a young couple push a stroller with twins. The stroller is a wobbly secondhand one. Mom would say that family wasn't wealthy, but they were rich in other ways. When I park in front of the Moriartys' house another car pulls up at the same time. Mr. Moriarty, I think.

I hurry over and introduce myself and hand him another one of the business cards that I poached from the little cardholder on the edge of Tracy Lee's desk.

The man gets out of his car and looks me up and down. "You work for a newspaper?" he says.

"Yes, the *North Bend Courier*," I say.

His gray eyes glide over me like a doctor's stethoscope. "You're pretty enough to be on TV. Forget that print crap. Print media's dying anyway. Yeah, TV would love you."

My skin crawls a little, but I give him my spiel about the grief article and he invites me inside.

Dan Moriarty is in his fifties, with the build and styling of a man much younger. He isn't wearing a hoodie or anything, but the sweatshirt that he's pulled over his taut muscular frame touts a skateboard brand—the same one that Caleb told me was the best on the planet. *No, the best in the universe.* Dan Moriarty's hair is black. A little too black, I think. I wonder if it is the same shade that I dunked my brother's hair into on the ferry. I break a slight smile when I remember the color's name.

Dark and Dangerous.

The interior of the house is at odds with Mr. Moriarty's impeccable appearance. Clutter. Dust. A trail of cast-off clothing, mostly gym attire, lines the hallway. I get it. As I suspected from my internet search at the library, there is no Mrs. Moriarty. Mr. Moriarty is at the tail end of his last gasp to get another woman. I know his type. I've seen those guys huffing and puffing at the gym or lurking in the wrong section in the mall. Getting their mojo back. Trying to score again. Whatever. When his eyes linger over my breasts—which really aren't much to linger over—my Creeper Meter goes to the top of the scale. My CM is seldom wrong. With this new haircut and anything other than jeans and a T-shirt attire that I'm wearing, I know that I do look, let's say, more available. Young. But definitely available. I'll go with it if I have to.

"Is Mrs. Moriarty home?" I ask, already knowing the answer.

He peels off the sweater, letting his abs show. I want to hurl like Marilee again, but I don't. I know he did that intentionally, like it was going to be some big turn-on. Accidental turn-on.

"She ran off. After Megan vanished. Complained that I wasn't 'emotionally' there for her. Whatever the hell that means."

I ignore the superior tone and the bitterness that he spits out with each word.

"That fits within the article I'm writing," I say. "The impact on people after such a tragedy is nearly insurmountable for some families, such as yours."

Oh my God. I just sounded like I was a pageant girl giving an airheaded speech. I'm hoping he's too self-absorbed to notice.

He is.

"You want a beer or something?"

I so don't.

"Love one," I say. "But only one. This story is very important to me, and to other families in your situation."

Why am I acting this way? Is it because this lecherous man keeps darting his snake tongue out at me?

Mr. Moriarty invites me to sit on the sofa while he goes in the kitchen to get the beer. I feel better now that he's gone. Like the Blumes, there is a shrine of sorts to Megan. Her pom-poms are draped over the mantle next to a large framed photograph in her full cheer regalia. She's on the top of the pyramid. *Of course.* I look at her with a mixture of sadness, a little envy, and curiosity. Cheerleaders are like a foreign species to me. I've never even talked to one. It's true that I've had a wall around me for as long as I can remember, a force field that's impenetrable by necessity. But in a way those girls do too. Their utter perfection, their veneer of narcissism is their barrier. Next to the photograph is a triptych—a word that I learned in Art class—showing the three phases of Megan's life. A baby swaddled in pink. A little girl swinging from the monkey bars at school. A cheerleader.

"She was very pretty," I say when Mr. Moriarty hands me an amber bottle of beer.

130

He swallows some beer, slumps into a chair across from me. I'm grateful for that. My CM indicated he'd slide next to me on the couch. I'm not always right.

For the next hour he drinks three beers. I dump the second half of mine in the plant on the stand next to me. It foams over and I'm pretty sure he's going to notice. But he doesn't. He's too busy telling me what a bitch his wife was and flexing his triceps in that way that is supposed to turn a girl on.

"Another beer?" he offers.

"I have to drive." I don't tell him that I barely know how to drive and that drinking any more than half a bottle of beer is too great of a risk. I can't get a DUI. If I did my mother would die of complete embarrassment.

Before my father actually kills her. If I don't find her in time.

Mr Moriarty tells me about the trial. How Megan's boyfriend, Kim Mock, was convicted.

"I wasn't sorry when he got shanked to death by some crazy in prison. I mean, not at first," says Mr. Moriarty. He belches and I do my best not to recoil.

I didn't know Kim had been killed, but I don't let on.

"Retribution," I offer instead. "For Megan?"

He nods. I see a strange look in his eyes. I can't quite place it.

"You're holding something back, Mr. Moriarty."

"Call me Dan, honey."

I resist the childish compulsion to call him Dan-Honey.

"Dan, what is it?"

He draws in a deep breath then exhales the warm air of a brewery in my direction. I try not to wince.

"I don't know. My wife. *Ex-wife.* She never really believed that Kim killed Megan. I guess I had some doubts too."

"What doubts?" I ask.

"Kim was a typical teenager. Sure, he was all over Megan like a dirty shirt half the time, but she could hold her own. She was a cheerleader, but she didn't put out. She told her mom she was saving herself for her husband. That's cool. That's every father's hope. I think Kim understood that. My ex didn't think he was the type to abduct and rape Megan. Anyone who really knew him said he wouldn't do that."

I take in his words. His demeanor has changed with the speed of a flash flood. He looks broken-hearted, pathetic. His wall has come down. I don't trust him, but in that moment I find something to like about him. He loved his daughter. He thought she was safe. He is awash with regret.

"Megan was missing for ten days, right?"

He shakes his head. "Two weeks."

"Where was Kim?"

"That's just it. He was here most of the time. He was helping to look for her. It didn't seem to any of us that he could fake that kind of hurt and worry. Kim was just as distraught as we were. Devastated." He stops and peels off the label on the beer bottle, then stares over in the direction of the mantel.

"Mr. Moriarty—I mean, Dan," I say, trying to reel him back in the moment. "You don't think Kim did it? Despite the evidence?"

He snaps back. His dark eyes look directly into mine. "I wanted to believe it. I really did. The detective working the case recovered Megan's underwear from Kim's car. Dirt in the trunk matched soil on her heels."

"Where did they say he kept her?"

This is important. I don't know for sure, of course, but I hope that wherever the killer kept Megan—the same place he kept my mother—is still a favorite.

Dan Moriarty shifts in his chair. "They never knew," he says. "Somewhere around here. I never figured Kim could do that to my little girl. Raping her. Defiling her like he did."

Part of me wants the gory details of what the killer did to Megan because I know that whatever it was—up to a point—was the same thing he did to my mom. *My mother*. They were all picked up around the same time. I look down at my notes. I see the date on which Megan disappeared. I calculate backwards nine months.

I am sixteen. *Sweet sixteen*. I'm the same age as the girls.

The thought of that brings me back to the tattoo. I ask Mr Moriarty if Megan had a tattoo.

"That's another thing," he says, surprised by my question. "Not many people know about that. We hadn't seen it before. They said she got it a week or so before she went missing."

My heart rate quickens. I already know what it was and where it was. I ask anyway.

"A heart. On her shoulder," he says.

"With a sixteen in it?"

He shoots me a peculiar look. "Yeah, how did you know?"

I turn to a clean page in the reporter's notebook—also stolen from cat-loving community newspaper editor Tracy Lee—and sketch out my recollection of the one Mom had on her shoulder. It was faint and I was so young, but I do my best to draw it anyway.

"Did it look like this?" I ask, spinning the notebook in his direction.

He nods slowly, very slowly, as though he's fighting a recollection that at once hurts and haunts. Then he dissolves into tears.

"Yeah. I only saw it one time. In a police photo."

BACK AT THE BEST WESTERN, I take an apple from the front desk and go to the business center. I hover over a kid playing *Candy Crush* and sigh loudly. He ignores me and goes on with his game until I do it a second and third time. Finally, and very reluctantly, he leaves the little room containing a single computer, a printer, and a trash can. I hold it inside, but I'm enraged. After seeing what my bio dad has done to the Blumes and even Dan Moriarty I want to kill him for that alone. What kind of human garbage goes around torturing young girls? What kind of evil ectoplasm coagulated to create this monster? I have a gun. I have an ice pick. I have scissors. I will need even more than those to come after him and put him in a place where he writhes in agony and I show him what it is to experience the pain he's brought to others. That's what's driving me. The mask that I've been wearing as I play Tracy Lee is starting to crack and I'm fully aware of it.

I search Kim Mock's name on the internet. It's a common name, but the one I'm looking for is the one that was incarcerated for Megan Moriarty's murder. I skim through the trial transcripts and news articles. Nothing more jumps out at me. I see a picture of Kim. He looks bewildered, sitting next to his defense attorney. In the background I see a man I recognize as Dan Moriarty—younger, but out of shape. Next to him is a woman with her hands pressed against her chest as if she's holding her breaking heart inside. Megan's mom. She has those same haunted eyes that I saw in Mrs. Blume. *No mother ever gets over such a loss.* If I was going to actually write that article as Tracy Lee that's how I would start it.

Next, I scroll down. A headline jumps at me.

MOCK SUCCUMBS TO INJURIES

I devour the article giving a recap of Kim Mock's crime. All of it. How he'd been sentenced to life, and how, on his eighteenth birthday, he was moved from a juvenile justice center in Seattle to the men's correctional facility in Monroe, a sleepy prison town east of Everett, Washington. As I read, it is as though I'm in a race to capture every detail I can in one giant gulp. He was considered a model prisoner there, teaching other inmates how to read and write. He even led a Bible study group.

On Tuesday Mock was in the prison chapel when an assailant stabbed him with a knife made from a flattened and sharpened spoon. Mock was taken to the infirmary where he died after surgery. His attacker has not been identified. The prison was on lockdown for twenty-four hours, but is operating normally again today.

At the bottom of the article mention is made that there was a pending investigation into Mock's death.

I move further down the computer screen. The article is so brief that if I blinked at the moment it passed in front of me I would have missed it.

REVIEW INTO MOCK DEATH COMPLETE

I can't see any of the words in an order that I can read because a person's name assaults my eyes. It pulses at me. It sends a shiver down my spine. At the same time I feel a kind of elation and hope. Just for a moment.

The name of the guard who found Kim Mock stabbed and alone was Michael Rader.

An icy chill pours down my body.

From what little I can find about Alex Rader, and there isn't much—no phone, no address—I know from an old directory still online that Alex has a younger brother. His name is Michael.

Chapter Twelve

Cash: $53.
Food: Four apples from the front desk. One granola bar.
Shelter: Best Western Motel, Kent, Washington.
Weapons: Gun, scissors, ice pick.
Plan: Find Alex Rader and shove the ice pick into his eyes.

AS I DRIFT INTO UNEASY slumber, Selma comes to me in a dream. The girl from the rest stop is running as fast as she can. Her feet are bare and bloody, her dark curls streaming back in the wind. I call out to her to hurry, but no sound comes from my lips. She moves toward me, and as she approaches, I recognize the look in her eyes. She's terrified of something and she needs my help. She screams. The sound is so loud that I close my eyes to try to seal it from my eardrums. When I snap them open a second later, still in my dream, all I see is a white and red nightgown laying in the parking lot next to the well-worn trail to the restroom. I cry out for Selma as I hurry to the nightgown. I pick it up and hold it to my face. The smell is unpleasant, and I know instantly what it is. I'm taking in the acrid odor of blood.

When I pull away, I notice that my hands are bloody.

The dream—no, the nightmare—propels me out of my restless slumber. I feel sick, scared, angry. I don't grasp the importance of the dream or why I had it. Caleb told me one time that dreams were messages from your subconscious. I'm more practical than that, but I let him believe that I agreed. I hated lying to him, but I saw the lie as a way to get just a little bit closer to him. So if he was right and I was wrong—and I don't like admitting it—what was that dream, that horrific dream, telling me? Was Selma me? Was Selma my mother? We're both blond, not dark haired. Our hair is straight, not the mass of curls of the girl running away from the van.

Then it begins to hit me. I roll out of the bed and go the bathroom where I sit on the toilet and cry. I am crying so loudly that I turn on the shower so that the people in the motel room next door can't hear. For good measure, I flush the toilet three times. In the mirror, I see my mother again. Not a ghost or a spirit or whatever, but the essence of her in my face. I don't say the words, but they move from my mind to wherever my mom is right now.

Hold on.

I'm coming.

I will make him pay with his life.

We will be free.

As I think these words, I know each one is a long shot. As resourceful as I want to be, I'm only fifteen—sixteen at the most. I'm a girl. I've never shot a gun or hurt anyone in my life. All the odds are against me except one thing that my bio dad could never count on.

I am determined to be as ruthless as he is.

THE NEXT MORNING I STEAL the maid's tip money from her supply cart parked in the middle of the hallway two rooms away. Honestly, she was almost offering it up as help for the cause. It was just sitting there out in the open and I took it. Crime of opportunity. I feel bad about it, of course, but I need enough cash for another night's lodging. That's in the immediate. I hurry past the tiny soaps and toilet paper-laden cart as silently and as quickly as I can to the front desk where I pay the clerk and say that my sister Leanne wants me to hang out with her one more day. I act put out by the inconvenience.

"I thought her name was Megan," she says.

Uh-oh.

"Megan-Leanne. I know," I say, "completely whack. My mother had two sisters and couldn't make up her mind so Meglee, as we sometimes call her, got stuck with a hyphenated name. I never know what to call her."

She shakes her head. "Parents can be so dumb."

I nod with a bemused look. "Yeah, and if you ask me," I say, "they don't get smarter with age."

That cracks her up and as I wait for her to print out the receipt I pick the lone banana from the remainder of the tragic little fruit bowl set aside for Diamond Members—of which I'm not, having never stayed there before. I don't really like bananas because they make my tongue feel itchy, but I'm getting tired of apples. A second later, I'm out the door and driving toward Leanne Delmont's childhood home in a neighborhood yet further south of Seattle in Tacoma. I'm pretty good at being a reporter, I think, and I wish that I'd taken more than three business cards from Tracy Lee's little holder. And it turns out that I'm not a halfway bad driver either. At least, no one is honking at me to go faster any more.

When I arrive my jaw drops. The Delmont residence grabs the edge of a cliff that overlooks the city of Tacoma and the surprisingly pristine looking waters of Commencement Bay. It is by far the biggest and nicest house that I've ever seen outside of a magazine. The front door is huge and all glass. I wonder how anyone could keep such a thing clean. Hayden with his dirty little fingers would make a mess of it in about two minutes.

Hayden. His third day alone. I worry about him. So small. So trusting. And I've abandoned him. I want to call him. I need to. But I can't. At least I don't think it is a good idea. I don't know if he and Aunt Ginger are really safe. I could be wrong about my father. He might be watching them too, as he tries to find me.

A woman with spun gold hair and big diamond earrings answers the door. I recognize her immediately. Leanne's mother, Monique Delmont, was in all the papers. After her daughter's disappearance and murder, she found purpose in creating and funding a victims' advocacy group that eventually led to more stringent laws against habitual offenders.

Like the monster that police and prosecutors said killed her only child.

This advocacy group had made life much easier for me. Last night I simply called their number from the motel and arranged to meet with Mrs. Delmont. She told me she'd be

140

happy to help with my article.

"We must never forget our victims and all they've gone through," she said before hanging up.

The gleaming hardwood floor echoes under the heels of her designer shoes as she leads me to a cozy seating area in the corner of a great room that is full of understated elegance. The room is larger than the last two houses our family lived in. She offers coffee and some amazing almond cookies and I am grateful for something other than fruit and granola bars. I know I should stop and have a proper meal, but I can't. I am running out of time.

She looks at me closely. The look on her face is strange. Sweet. Concerned. I haven't seen that kind of look in my direction in a long time. If I have, I didn't acknowledge it. I keep the shell pretty secure.

"Are you all right, dear?" she asks.

I wonder what it is that she thinks is wrong with me.

"Excuse me?" I say in the kindest, most nonthreateningly, attitude-free manner in which anyone could ever utter that pair of words.

Her eyes are deep blue and full of genuine concern. She looks down at my hands. "You've chewed your nails to the quick," she says.

I look down. My fingernails *are* nearly gone. I hadn't realized that I'd been gnawing them to the point of oblivion. I wonder what other ways my anger, anxiety, fear, and need for revenge is manifesting itself. I feel I am changing in ways that I both welcome and revile. Chewed nails are on the reviled side of the T-chart that makes up my life's pros and cons.

"It's just this story," I say, noticing that one of my fingertips is wet. Have I been chewing my nails in front of her? How could I be so unaware of myself? What *is* wrong with me?

"It has been a long time, but it still hurts me deeply too. I try to keep busy. I try to help, but in the background I still see my Leanne and her father on the sailboat, smiling, having the time of their lives. She went missing from the marina and I play that day over and over."

"Of course you already know this because of your work, but you're not alone. All homicide survivors feel that way." As the words tumble from my lips, I notice her face tighten. I was trying to be thoughtful, but it came off as condescending. I reel back in my words with the only thing that I can think of. I lie to her.

"My sister Courtney was murdered," I say. "I grieve for her every day."

Monique Delmont's face relaxes. She rests her hands on my knee. "Well then, we're in a sisterhood of unending grief," she says.

I don't want to be in any such sisterhood. I want to be in a sisterhood of vengeance and retribution. All of her meetings, her fundraisers, her local talk show appearances, haven't added up to anything. Not really. As long as the killers breathe in the same air as we do, victims' families are never free.

We talk about the article I'm supposedly writing and then burrow into the specifics of her case. Apart from the reference to the sailboat, Mrs. Delmont doesn't mention her husband once in our time together. I don't know if they're divorced or if he's dead. I don't ask. I don't think I can take one more bit of the hurt that visits the parents of dead children.

Her gaze is directed out at the waters of Commencement Bay and the tankers and the parade of tugboats that plow through its deep blue waters. She talks about the hell that became her world when Leanne disappeared and was found twenty-two days later in a gravel pit and quarry near Issaquah, Washington. It was hard to pin down exactly what had killed her because there were so many attacks on her body. She'd been beaten. Burned. Stabbed. The medical examiner who testified at trial said that what had been done to the sixteen-year-old was "the most heinous and barbaric attack" she'd ever seen inflicted upon another human being.

When I deplete her tray of cookies, she gets more. She is as nice as she's beautiful and my questions, I have no doubt, are torturous at best. It's like pulling the wings off a baby bird, but I carry on. I need to find out what my mother saw in terms of a link between her abduction, Megan's, Shannon's, and Leanne's.

As I already know, the case was attributed to Arnold Cantu, a serial killer who plagued the Pacific Northwest for more than a decade. Like many of his kind, Cantu preyed on a particular type of victim—the blonde, slender, pretty. Leanne was the youngest of his victims and the only one not abducted from a college campus in his murder-spree—a spree that spanned eight terrifying years. At first, Mr. and Mrs. Delmont resisted the notion that their Leanne had been brutalized and killed by Cantu. She was too young. She wasn't a college student. When it came out that there had been a period of time when Leanne had run away from home and crashed at a house not far from the University of Washington campus in Seattle, they stopped their insistence that she did not fit Cantu's victim profile and began their focus on victims' rights.

"Those were really hard times for us, dear," she says. "I was embarrassed about some of Leanne's choices and I didn't want the world to think I was a bad mother. I made it sound as though she was a selfish, indulgent girl who didn't follow rules whatsoever. Now I am revolted by my characterization of my daughter, but that's how I felt. She was a wild girl from a privileged background. She never thought of anyone but herself."

Her heels play like raindrops as she walks over to a portrait of her daughter. It's propped on the grand piano among other family pictures.

"This is the last photo we ever took of her," she says. Her tone is wistful. She runs her fingers along a thick braid of gold chains that flow from her neckline.

For the first time, I notice Mrs. Delmont's fingernails are bitten too.

I gently, reverently, touch the edge of the gilded frame.

"She was beautiful."

And she was. In the photo, Leanne Delmont sits on a massive driftwood log at Point Defiance Park, an irony not lost on her mother. Or me. She looks over her right shoulder at the camera with a wary, but somewhat shy pose.

I move my gaze from the photo to Mrs. Delmont.

"When did you say this was taken?" I ask.

She takes a breath, remembering. "The week she went missing. She and her father moored off the point and took the skiff in for a picnic."

I take a deep breath. Then I ask, "Did she have a tattoo?"

Mrs. Delmont looks at me with a searing gaze.

"How did you know that?" she asks.

"I don't know," I say. "I just wondered."

She knows I'm lying, but she doesn't press me for more.

"Yes, that awful tattoo. A heart with a 16. She must have gotten it right before she disappeared. Barely healed. I haven't thought about it in years. Of course, no one knew about it. Another girl, years ago, called me about that very thing. I don't know why, but I denied it."

I get up to leave. It's an awkward retreat. But I know that the other girl who called her was my mother. I know that Leanne's killer had marked all of his victims. It was gross and disgusting like the way a dog pees on a bush to remind others that the shrubbery is his domain.

"Just who are you?" Monique Delmont asks as I ricochet my way from the great room to the front door.

I don't answer. Not because I'm rude or ill mannered. But because I don't really know.

Chapter Thirteen

Cash: $20.
Food: Three apples and a banana from the front desk. Six or seven almond cookies.
Shelter: Best Western Motel, Kent, Washington.
Weapons: Gun, scissors, ice pick.
Plan: Get a grip on what I need to do.

THE RED MESSAGE LIGHT BLINKS at me as I throw myself on the bed neatly made by the woman I stole tip money from this morning. That doesn't feel particularly good. As the events of the day sink in, I know one thing for certain—I cannot stay here another night. Despite the fact that I've already paid for the room, I have to get on the move. I need to find Alex Rader. I'm all but certain that Mom's carefully scattered breadcrumbs have taken me as far as I can go. I know now without any trace of doubt that the three girls plus Mom were linked by the actions of a very sick man. *My father.* I get that. I don't need to run around playing reporter to find out any more about that. There's nothing to find. I ignore the blinking light as I lay out my weapons. The gun, the bullets—those were gifts from Mom. I also have the scissors I bought at the drug store in Port Orchard; the ice pick taken from my aunt's house. Joining my pitiful arsenal is a bottle of Xanax that I liberated from Monique Delmont's medicine cabinet when I used her bathroom. It isn't a poison and I can't imagine exactly how the drug would help me when I intend to put a bullet through the very center of bio dad's forehead.

Maybe the Xanax is something I need for myself?

In order to kill him, I have to know where he lives. I unfold the Western Washington map taken from the brochure rack in the lobby. I already know that Alex Rader is not listed in any online directory—somehow he's managed to elude any kind of an internet trail. I'm guessing that's because he's connected to law enforcement and they have people on staff to—in the irony of all ironies—ensure that he's safe from the creeps he's sent to prison.

I go over the events as I know them.

Shannon was taken on Saturday, July 6th and found ten days later, on Tuesday, July 16th. She had been dead for a while—maybe as long as three days.

Megan was taken on Saturday, July 13th, and her body was found twelve days later, on July 25th, a Thursday. She had been dead a few days.

Leanne was likely taken on Saturday, July 20th and her body was found twenty-two days later, on August 11th, a Sunday. She was pretty badly decomposed, likely a result of the warm weather that hit the Seattle area. I'd seen another article from the same date when scanning the material online at the North Bend library. It featured a Bellevue couple that had painted

147

their brown lawn green in protest at HOA restrictions on watering in their exclusive neighborhood.

It passes through my mind that some people have no ability to measure what's truly important. I'm not sure I do, but I think I'm on the right track.

It dawns on me then that I don't know for sure when Mom was abducted, but I know it had to be *after* Leanne's vanishing. I'm thinking Saturday, July 27th. Alex Rader, it seems, had kept his Saturdays very busy during that particular month of July. In addition, I think that there may have been an overlap in the victims. I remembered Mom's note about Leanne with a shiver.

I saw her.

Maybe Mom wasn't the only one who saw another girl wherever it was that he'd kept them?

WHEN I CAN NO LONGER avoid the staccato strobe of the blinking light, I pick up the phone and it goes to voicemail immediately.

"Ms. Lee, this is Debra Blume. I was going to try your office number, but I remembered you said you were staying at the Best Western. I need you to call me back as soon as you get this message."

The tone in her voice is anything but calm.

I dial the number she leaves at the end of her message.

"Mrs. Blume?" I ask, when she answers on the first ring, trying to keep my ever-increasing anxiety on my side of the phone line.

I might need that Xanax after all.

She says hello and then launches into the reason for the call.

Her words seem off a little, like she's unsure if she should be calling. Or, I think, like she's afraid to call.

"I don't know if this will be helpful," she says, "but something strange happened this afternoon."

I'm hanging on every word, but I don't urge her on. She's going to get where she's going as soon as she can. She's a little unnerved. I hope her husband is okay, though I don't know why I would think she'd call me to tell me that.

"After you left, that detective I was telling you about called."

My heart sinks. He's following me.

"The one whose name you couldn't recall?" I ask.

"Yes, that's the one. Alex Rader. He's the one from the sheriff's office. Anyway, he came to our house and asked me questions about *you*. He told me that you were an imposter bent on stirring up trouble."

My pulse quickens at the mention of his name. Alex Rader is trailing me. Who will find who first? Seems like my biological father and I are in a kind of competition to see who can find the other. I intend to win. I *have* to win.

"I wonder why he said that?" I finally say as though the accusation seems incomprehensible, when deep down I know it is an astute observation. The truth is that I have been an imposter my entire life. But so has he. He's lived among the shadows, doing evil at night. During the day, he masquerades as an upstanding citizen. A cop. I know that he's killed all those girls. Maybe others. I know he has my mother right now. I just don't know where.

"You didn't tell him where I was?" I ask, trying to hold the heaving of my heart inside my ribcage.

"Oh no," she answers. "I never trusted or liked him whatsoever. Neither did my husband. He was nothing more than a conceited snot that never gave one whit about Shannon. He said all the right words, but I knew he was just a climber looking for a notch on his detective shield."

"I know the type all too well," I say, as I cradle the phone and look over my weapons. "Such a fraud."

"I wanted you to know that he's after you."

And I'm after *him*.

"Thank you, Mrs. Blume," I say doing my best impression of a warm and unworried tone. "I appreciate that."

She thanks me and ends our conversation with, "I could tell when we talked that you care about Shannon."

Though unintended, her words are a dagger to my heart. I know she means to comfort me, but I don't care about Shannon. I don't care about anything other than finding my mom and killing my bio dad. Now *he's* tracking me. I guess it wouldn't be hard. He probably knew what car Aunt Ginger drove. He might have followed her to see my mother, watching her afar that Labor Day when the two sisters met under the arches at the Pacific Science Center in Seattle. Maybe a police traffic camera caught the plates of the Ford Focus? It wouldn't be hard to find me. As careful as I've been.

I hang up. My heart's pressing harder against my ribcage. I'm only certain of one thing. I have to leave. First I go downstairs to the front desk and tell the clerk that my suitcase is jammed and I need a screwdriver to get into the lock. She pulls one from the top drawer and hands it to me. I go outside, looking north, then south in the parking lot. It is empty. I hurry over to the car closest to mine and remove my Idaho plates. I remove the plates from a blue Dodge caravan, hoping the mother and father will be so distracted by their brood that they won't notice their missing license plates until long after I'm gone. After screwing their plates on the Focus, I toss the Idaho plates into the trash and return to my room to get my things. I already paid for tonight's stay, but I can't remain here.

Exactly two minutes later I'm on the road.

Chapter Fourteen

Cash: $20.
Food: Nothing.
Shelter: The car.
Weapons: Gun, scissors, ice pick, bottle of Xanax, screwdriver.
Plan: Pour gas on my dad's body and light him on fire. Not really. But something dark inside me tells me that would be permissible. Maybe even fun.

A DENNY'S RESTAURANT SIGN BECKONS. I haven't eaten a real meal since Aunt Ginger's place in Wallace. My eyes look hollow and I know that's a symptom of both hunger and my escalating anxiety. I find a spot at the counter next to an old man nursing a hangover. I spread out the map with Xs indicating where Alex Rader's victims were last seen and found. When a heaping platter of scrambled eggs, silver dollar pancakes, and a rasher of bacon arrive, I devour it all. If heaven was real and if it had a flavor, it would be bacon swimming in maple syrup. I order coffee too. I let the hot drink roll down into my stomach slowly. Caffeine will help. When the man next to me leaves, I reach for his butter-stained newspaper.

And immediately I see my face. My old face, that is. The face I had before I did the Mom makeover. The headline makes me nearly toss my breakfast up on the counter, but I manage to keep it in my stomach.

KITSAP TEEN WANTED FOR QUESTIONING IN FATHER'S
MURDER INQUIRY

I read the article in the Seattle paper—the same paper I was mad at for denying my stepfather's murder any coverage—and I'm completely aghast. The story indicates that evidence at the scene has led to the case being investigated as patricide—murder of a father by his child. While investigators couldn't rule out the missing wife and mother, there were indications that "the daughter was deeply troubled and showed signs of rage."

. . . Caradee Hagen, a sophomore at the high school and close friend of the missing teenager, indicated that Rylee Cassidy was "a strange loner. She really never had anything to say. She kind of just clung to the background. Probably waiting and plotting."

Another student, Marilee Watson, said that Cassidy was often seen in the school bathroom. "She was always in there, sulking around. I hope they find her soon because, well, I don't know that she's a killer but I do know that she never, ever talked about her family. She must have really hated them."

One student had a different view. Caleb Hunter said that Cassidy was just another misunderstood teenager.

"Rylee is a lot of things, but she's not evil. Not at all," he said.

Caleb was always there for me. He still is.

The article concluded with a mention that an anonymous tip to the Crime Stoppers police-line changed the course of the investigation.

Said a police spokesperson: "We were thinking that it was a homicide and abduction. That's not the case right now."

I sit there in stunned silence. The cooks in the serving window between the kitchen and the counter move in slow motion. The lights above me rise further away and darkness overtakes me. I don't know for how long. I don't really know what happened. I hear someone speaking but I can barely register what he or she is saying.

"Lady! Are you all right?"

It's a young man's voice. A teenager. His voice crackles a little.

I open my eyes. I'd reached overload. I'd blacked out. The idea that I could hurt my family and that those awful so-called friends would say those things about me was like a sucker punch to the gut.

"I'm pregnant," I quickly say. "Just a blood-sugar imbalance. Or hormonal."

The kid turns a shade of red I haven't seen since the year Mom and I pickled beets.

"You need a doctor?" he asks.

I shake my spinning head. "No. More coffee, please."

He disappears to the cof.ee station and I pull myself together. I know damn well who the anonymous tipster was. There's no denying it. *Alex Rader*. Has to be. That twisted piece of garbage is toying with me. He knows I'm looking for him.

When the busboy returns and fills my cup, I point at my purse.

"My phone's dead. I think I should call my doctor. I'm worried about the baby. I've never fainted like that before."

"Uh—sure," he says. "My parents put me on some mega plan and I never use all my minutes. Have at it."

I'm going to give that kid a really good tip.

He hands me his phone and says it's not password protected.

"Call's kind of personal," I say. "I'm going to use it in the bathroom."

"Uh. Okay."

It's a unisex rest room, of the type that I normally loathe for the same reason I hate sharing a bathroom with Hayden. His habit of not flushing and dribbling on the toilet seat seems to be a guy thing that starts at an early age. From the unisex bathrooms I've visited, it doesn't get better with practice. I flip the lock. I know that I have an advantage over other people. I am very good with remembering numbers. Most kids I know can't even call a friend from any phone but their own. Apparently, they have no capacity to store information like that. I think of the time that Caradee couldn't phone Gemma because she'd left her phone at home, and nearly lost it in the school cafeteria. Thinking of them brings me right back to the article I just read.

Caradee. That bitch. Marilee that fountain-puker. They both trashed me good in the paper.

I fume a little as I dial Aunt Ginger's number, which is a bit of a wild card. I've never called her before, but I can see the digits on the slip of paper she gave me with the ten twenties.

155

She answers.

"It's me. Rylee."

"Where are you?" she asks, desperation in her voice. "They are looking for you. I saw on the news. They say you did it."

I'm surprised that she already knew. For the past couple of days I've been running around so much, trying to figure out why and what Alex Rader did sixteen years ago, that I didn't stay current on what was going on at the moment.

"I know," I say, not adding that I just found out fifteen seconds ago. "I'm okay."

"Have you found your mother?" Ginger asks.

"No. Not yet."

I'm not on the phone for chitchat and I have another call to make before I give the phone back to the red-faced busboy at the Denny's counter.

"Did Mom have a tattoo?" I ask before Aunt Ginger tries to work in a topic of her own.

A beat of silence fills my ear.

Aunt Ginger exhales.

"Yes," she says. "That's one of the things he did to her. Not one of the worst things, but one that was meant to be a lasting reminder."

Like me. That's what I am. A reminder too.

"What day did she disappear?" I ask, moving on. "Do you know?"

"I'll never forget. Saturday, July twenty-seventh."

I was right but I don't say so.

"Is Hayden there?" I ask.

"Yes, of course."

I hear her hand the phone to my little brother.

"Rylee, did you find Mom?"

"Not yet," I say. "I will."

"You promise," he says, a pleading tone in his voice.

"Yes," I answer. "A true promise."

Hearing his voice makes me tear up a little. He's so trusting. He doesn't understand half of what is going on. All he knows is that our mom is gone, our dad is dead, and I'm trying to bring Mom home safely.

"When will you be home?"

I'm not sure. I don't even know where home is anymore. Aunt Ginger's, I guess. Hayden is used to "the switch" so he thinks wherever we stay awhile is our new home.

"Soon," I say. "As soon as I find Mom."

He starts to cry.

"Hayden, it'll be okay. I need you to be good and tough and strong. I'm depending on you."

He fights his tears and I let him catch his breath. I don't try to fill his ears with more promises, things that I can never make true.

"For what?" he asks. "What can I do?"

"Nothing now, but later. I'm depending on you to help me and Mom when we get home," I say. "Especially Mom. She'll be counting on you just as I am right now. You're the man of the house."

He sniffs a little and says something about promising to do whatever we need him to do. But he's only seven and that's a tall order, I think.

"Love you," I say, a phrase that I have now said to him on two occasions.

"I love you too," he says back.

Aunt Ginger takes the phone.

"Be careful," she says. "Remember, don't trust the police. That much I know for sure."

I tell her that I don't trust anyone. That includes her, but I don't have much of a choice right now.

I hang up and take a breath. The keypad stares up at me. I start with the area code 360 and my chewed-to-the-nub fingertip dials the rest of it.

"Hey?" Caleb's voice answers.

I am mute. I don't know why. Maybe it's the fact that I just talked to my brother and his little voice was full of urgency and hope? Tears start down my cheeks and I hear a knock on the door. My heart rate escalates and I pull the phone from my mouth and call out to the intruder.

"Please give me a minute!"

I look down through my tears as I hear him speak.

"Rylee?" he asks. "Is that you?"

My finger hovers over the button to hang up, but I can't. Not yet. I've never had the chance to say goodbye. I don't know what will happen to me when all of this plays out. I don't know if I'll find my mom and kill my bio dad or if he'll find and kill me. I don't know if I'll be arrested and convicted of my father's murder. I don't know anything for sure.

"Yes," I say. My voice feels bunched up. Tight. Like the words are literally jammed deep into my airway and I can only cough them out, one at a time.

"Where are you?" he asks. "Are you all right? I know you didn't do anything."

"Caleb, I . . . I just wanted to tell you that I'm sorry. That I lied to you."

There is a long silence, and for a minute I think he has hung up on me. Then he speaks, his voice quiet but imploring.

"What do you mean, you lied to me?"

"About who I am," I say as I pick through the landmine of excuses, of lies, of truths that I could tell him. "About *what* I am."

"I don't understand," he says.

My tears hit the top of the bathroom faucet and slide into the sink. I wonder if I could fill the basin.

"I don't really either," I say, gathering myself a little. "I just wanted you to know that out of a lifetime of deception you were the only thing that was real to me."

I don't wait to hear his response. *I can't.* I hang up. My words to him just then were the truth. But half of what I said to him face to face was a lie. I betrayed him because I figured he was like the others—someone who would fade into the background of a life on the run. There had been others. But no boys. He was the only boy that really mattered.

I splash water on my face. When I look in the mirror it is with a renewed resolve. I take a deep breath. Another. I've sufficiently pulled myself together. At least I hope so. When I open the door a little boy doing the pee dance rushes past me.

"I'm really sorry," I say, words that aren't really directed at the hotfooted kid, but at Caleb Hunter.

I get back to my place at the counter and return the cellphone. I look down at the map where I've placed my water glass. I get an idea.

Actually, two.

Chapter Fifteen

Cash: $20.
Food: No need.
Shelter: The car.
Weapons: Gun, scissors, ice pick, bottle of Xanax, screwdriver.
Plan: Track him now.

THE WATER GLASS. CONDENSATION FROM the restaurant's moist air collected on its surface, leaving a ring of water on the map. I fish a pen out of my stolen purse and set the glass over the spot where Shannon was last seen and I run the ink around the base of the glass. I do the same thing with Megan, Mom, and Leanne. I don't know for sure, but something tells me that Alex Rader was a lazy predator. The dumpsites of each of his victims were not far from the location of their abductions. I suspect that he had to live somewhere in the vicinity of where he'd done his hunting. Dogs are not supposed to crap in their kennel but I think so little of Alex Rader that I have it in my mind that *he* most likely did.

The water glass—well, not the glass itself, but its contents—give me the second idea.

The kid with the phone comes back. I put down $15 for the $6 meal and tell him to keep the change.

"You don't have to do that," he says, quickly reaching for the cash.

I wave my hands at the money, letting him know that he should take what he's already snatched up.

"I really appreciate the use of your phone," I say. "The doctor warned me to take better care of myself and told me to get some homeopathic vitamins. Do you know where Nature To Go is?"

He narrows his brow and shakes his head.

I make a disappointed face. "Mind if I look it up on your phone?"

With the money in his pocket, he doesn't hesitate. "Sure," he says, sliding it across the sticky counter. I open a browser window and locate the water utility that services the area where the rings intersect.

Suburban Water District No. 4—a dot in the dead center.

Dead center.

That's where I intend to shoot Alex Rader.

I return the phone and take the map. Fifteen minutes later, I arrive at the utility's address. A woman named Sue is helping a customer. Actually, trying to quiet a customer. It seems that his water's been cut off and he has no money for a connection fee and a back bill. She tells him there's a "Sunshine" fund and he can apply for assistance. The man is in his twenties, wearing an oily pair of jeans and tousled brown hair that could definitely use the benefits of shampoo. He wants no sunshine. He slams a fist on the counter and Sue sighs as he storms out of the place.

"Good timing," I say. "I'm here to help out my neighbor.

161

They've run into some financial problems and I want to pay their water bill. You know, a kind of neighbor-to-neighbor Sunshine fund."

She smiles and lets out weary breath.

"People do it all the time," she says. "You know, summer water consumption is at a year-long high and demand spikes the cost. Nice of you to help out—especially with you being so young, and all. Wish more people did that than come in here and complain to me. I don't set the price, you know. I only work here."

I nod at her when the phone rings.

She glances at me and lets out another sigh. Sue the Sigher is how I'll remember her. "Short staffed today. Short staffed every day," she says. "You'd think with what we charge for water we'd pay enough around here to keep more people from leaving for better paying jobs."

I nod like I care. But I don't. I care about only one thing right now.

The phone continues to ring.

"Name on the account?" she asks, with another sigh. I can imagine that it is more than the low-paying wage that keeps people from sticking around Sue.

"Rader, Alex," I chirp, as though an upbeat attitude would rub off on this Eeyore of a woman who rolls on her chair from her computer to the phone on the other side of her desk like a sidewinding crab. She puts the super-irate caller on hold.

Sue clacks out the name on her keyboard. I lean closer but I can't read the screen. She has one of those privacy screens covering it—as though water was such a secret elixir and its users must be protected.

"Right here, Alex and Marie Rader." She looks up at me with a strange look on her face. "But they're current."

"Really?" I say. "Are you sure it's them?"

She nods. "2424 Summer Hill Road?"

I shake my head. "I'm so embarrassed. I must have the wrong neighbor. I just assumed it was the Raders that were having problems."

"Nope," she says. "Never a second late."

I thank her. She sighs again and I hurriedly retreat to my car. My heart is pumping a little faster. Alex Rader, you bastard, I'm coming for you. You think you can hide. You think your policeman cronies can cover your tracks? You think you can hide from Google? From the water company?

Like all living things, you need water.

But not for much longer.

I APPROACH THE SUMMER HILL ROAD address provided by Sue the Sigher. It wasn't what I expected at all. As I ease Aunt Ginger's car past the neatly manicured lawns, the hedges sculpted to Disney perfection, I am dumbfounded at my own foolishness. Somehow I had expected Alex Rader to live out in the country in some dank little hideaway, not in a suburban development. I thought he'd be holed up in some, well, dank *hole* somewhere. This scene is so utterly ordinary. It's so benign. The Rader home is a two-story blue and white Cape Cod with dormers that are in perfect scale with the rest of the house—not a kind of architectural afterthought Mom deplored whenever we settled into a new rental.

"If we're not going to stay long, we might as well stay in a place that has some appeal. Being on the run doesn't mean we have to live like we're homeless," she said to me one time.

And yet, I always knew we *were* homeless. Not houseless.

A basketball hoop hangs over the Raders' garage. Since they don't have children, at least as far as I know from my internet searches, I imagine that Rader himself played there. The thought of his severed head going through the hoop crosses my mind. I don't know why, but it does. An apple tree laden with hundreds of green apples stands next to an arbor that almost looks supported by the massive wisteria vine that encircles it. I think how the vines might be wrapped around his neck as I gag him with an apple, like a roasted pig. He *is* a pig, I think, which is a total insult to real pigs. My eyes quickly scan the rest of the house. It is well cared for. It is unremarkable in every single way but one.

A cement ramp runs parallel with the steps to the front door. Someone who lives at 2424 Summer Hill Road needs the benefit of a wheelchair. I hope that it is the man, or rather, the scumbag of the house, but I know better. My money, what's left of it, is on Marie, his wife.

I bring the lost cat poster that I yanked from the community board at the library the day I stole the reporter's business cards. The flyer is a prop too. I know that props can be everything to a successful lie. It isn't necessarily the prop itself, but the illusion that something tangible provides. I remember the time Mom kept men's work boots by the front door before Rolland came into our lives. She actually muddied them a little every once in a while and stamped a few footprints onto the entryway.

She also draped a hunting jacket over the back of a chair and she moved the thick, heavy garment now and then.

Illusion.

It was the same thing I've seen neighbors do with the lights they set on automatic timers whenever they went on vacation. They wanted to create the impression that they were home. My mom wanted someone—and now I know who that someone has always been—to think there was some big, strong hunter in our house, protecting her.

Protecting me.

I draw a deep breath and steady myself before I make one more pass past the Rader residence. My instincts tell me the cover of darkness would be smarter, but I'm doing a daylight recon because there isn't any time to waste. I park and get out. A woman next door to the Raders is watering her fuchsia baskets and calls over to me. She's in her late fifties, I guess, though it's actually kind of hard for me to determine just how old someone is once they are on the far side of their thirties. That whole middle section is difficult. She's heavyset with Kool-Aid red hair and a sunhat that might be perfectly functional but it and her bad hair make her look like a second grader's dream of a circus clown.

"May I help you?" she says. Her tone is a little hard so I know I have to lay it on thick to win her over.

"Looking for my lost cat," I say, putting on a sad face. "I live a few blocks that way." I wave in some vague direction and hope she's just a busybody or helpful at best, and not the neighborhood-watch captain.

I approach and flash the flyer.

"Name?" she asks, still a little coolly.

I almost say Rylee, but then I realize the woman wants the name of the cat.

"Thor," I say, repeating the name on the flyer. I kind of like the ridiculousness of the missing cat's name. So much better than Mr. Fluffy or something along those lines. If I had a cat, I might actually name it Thor.

Boy or girl.

"He's pretty tough for a cat," I say, "but even so we're worried."

She squints into the sun and examines the flyer. "Haven't seen him. You should put a notice on Craigslist or in the 'Lost' section of the newspaper."

I pull the paper away. In case I need it again. I only have one flyer.

"They do those for free, right?" I say, straining to look past her to the garage next door. The Raders' garage. It's a two-car garage with a large window that runs the length of it. And from where I'm standing, it appears one car is missing. Next to this empty space is a large, bronze-colored van.

"I thought I'd knock on a few doors. To get the word out. I guess no one's home next door," I say.

She shuts off her hose. "Marie's home," she says. "She's always home. Unless her husband takes her somewhere, which isn't all that often. Maybe once a month. And that's if she's lucky."

The words come from her mouth, leaving her looking as though she's eaten something foul.

I go with it.

"Is she disabled?" I ask, indicating the ramp.

The woman nods and prepares to whisper a reply—her manner and tone suggest that she likes to tell the story, though she pretends not to.

"Car accident, years ago," she says, rolling the hose a little and moving to another plant. "It's really kind of a sad story."

I know without a doubt that she's not going to make me beg for it. This watering woman lives for this kind of gossip. She pretends to be sad, concerned, but really she enjoys gossiping so much that she cannot hide the slight smile that curls the corners of her mouth.

"What happened?" I ask anyway.

She stops what she's doing and shakes her head.

My heart is thumping, but I stand there casually. I want nothing more than to know everything I can about Alex and Marie Rader.

She tugs at the hose, stuck on a rock. "High school sweethearts, those two," she says. "Promise rings and all of that. Alex is a couple years older. Marie was a competitive swimmer. Stanford University scouted her. Anyway, he takes her to a kegger out in Issaquah to celebrate her birthday and well, you can almost guess the rest."

She doesn't make me guess, of course. I have a hunch as to what will follow. And I see no need to ask what birthday Marie was celebrating.

"Anyway," she goes on, "he got drunk and wanted to drive home. She insisted that he give her the keys but he told her to take a hike or something like that. I mean, not literally. Anyway, halfway home on the Issaquah-Hobart Road the car rolls and she ends up paralyzed. Waist down. Can't have kids."

167

The last three words are uttered with an extra dose of sympathy, to ensure that I understand that this lady next door is very concerned and definitely on Team Marie.

"That's terrible," I say. "So sad."

She nods. "Yes it is. Beyond terrible. He married her out of shame or guilt or something. I don't think he ever really loved her. Treats her like a doormat on wheels." She stops herself and assesses me. Her eyes run over mine. "I don't know what it is about you, but you've really got a way of making me open up. I feel like I'm really talking out of school here."

A can opener could open her up. That is, just *looking* at one.

"You're very nice," I say. "The lady—Marie—she's lucky to have you as a neighbor. Sounds like she could use a friend. You know, given all that she's been through."

She crosses her arms and pauses. She's pretending to hold back. I wait only a beat.

"You don't even know the half of it," she says. "I'm not saying this to be unkind or anything, but you've got me going big time and I just can't stop. Alex is a cop with the King County Sheriff's Office. So you'd think he'd be more discreet."

I'm not sure what she means and I'm not sure how to frame a question to ask. Of course, I don't have to.

"He used to come and go at all hours of the night," she says. She should be a newscaster. Or at the very least run some kind of online blog. Her strange clown-like appearance would undoubtedly make her a YouTube star. "Seeing prostitutes," she goes on, no longer feigning to struggle with the shade she's throwing on her neighbor. She hates him. That means I like her.

"Ladies of the night, or whatever," she goes on. "My husband calls them sluts. I saw Alex Rader walk a girl into the house one time late at night. Looked like she'd had a drink or two. I bet poor Marie had to listen to them go at it all night. Frank—that's my husband—says that I should cut him some slack because he's married to an invalid and men have needs. That's bullshit. Excuse me. But it is."

Finally she's done.

I'm not sure if I want to probe for more information or throw up into her fuchsia basket.

"Like I said, Marie's lucky you're here to watch out for her."

She acknowledges this with a faint smile, which quickly fades with her next words.

"You can tell I don't like him," she says. "But really, Marie's a doll. She deserves so, so much better."

I need to get moving. I need to get into that house next door.

"Do you think it would be all right if I knock on her door and ask about Thor?" I ask.

She doesn't hesitate. "Oh yes. By all means. Marie loves animals. She has a big koi pond in the backyard so she'd probably like to know, to make sure Thor doesn't mess with her finny friends. Be nice for Marie to have some company. I was going to go over later, but I'm running out of time. I'm going on vacation tomorrow. Got to get these plants watered before I leave—don't trust the kid across the street to do it properly."

AS I TURN TO LEAVE, the smile that has been plastered on my face evaporates. Fuchsia lady gave me more than I hoped, but honestly, I didn't think she'd ever shut up. The last thing

I need right now is for Alex Rader to come home and find me standing in the neighbor's yard getting a blow by blow of his sex life. I don't believe for one minute that he was carrying a prostitute into the house. I have the feeling deep in my bones that the limp girl in his arms was one of his victims. I just don't know which one.

Going up to the Raders' door, I plant my knuckles under an old-fashioned grapevine wreath affixed to the bright white front door and knock four times. In my head I'm thinking of the names of the girls I'm certain Alex Rader has killed. Shannon. Leanne. Megan. The fourth knock is for my mother, whom I pray is still alive. I know that Marie Rader gets around with the aid of a wheelchair so I resist what would be my next inclination. I don't punch the bell ten times to rouse her.

The knob finally turns and the door swings wide open. I drop my gaze to meet the woman in a wheelchair in front of me. She has blond hair. Her eyes are blue. I lower my flyer so that it is at her eye level.

"I'm sorry to bother you," I say. "I'm looking for my cat."

She eyes me warily.

"I saw you talking to Rachel," she says. "I thought you might be selling something and I was going to point to the sign." She indicates a little wooden placard next to the door.

No salespeople

I shake my head as I acknowledge it. "Sorry. I didn't see it."

"Everybody's always trying to sell me something," Marie says. "No, I haven't seen any cat."

I look past her to see if there's anything I can glean from her hallway, though it passes through my mind that I might want to just grab the handles of her wheelchair and push her into the nearest chasm. I could so do that. If I thought she knew what her husband had been doing with those girls.

"How old are you?" Marie asks.

Her words catch me off guard.

"I'm eighteen," I lie. "Why do you ask?"

She pushes back in her chair. "I was thinking about the time my cat was lost. I was younger than you. At least three years younger. I canvassed all the neighborhoods in the area, carrying a stuffed toy that resembled Abby."

A sad look overtakes her face.

"You never found her," I say, mirroring her expression. "Did you?"

She shakes her head. "No. She'd crawled into the undercarriage of the neighbor's car. We found her remains coiled up inside. I think she froze to death."

Marie had let her guard down and I knew it.

"I'm sorry," I say. "I can tell you really loved Abby. I don't know what I'll do if Thor doesn't come home."

She nods understandingly. "I was making some ice tea . . . " she says, leaving a pause at the end, a placeholder for my name.

"Tracy. Tracy Lee."

"Would you like to have a glass, Tracy? Hot out there today."

I suddenly feel sorry for her. Married to a monster. Confined to a wheelchair. Lonely enough to invite a stranger inside for a little company. She spins around and negotiates the living room with a speed and assuredness that I did not expect. Just

171

because she's in a wheelchair, doesn't make her a complete invalid. Before I turn my attention to my surroundings I notice two more things. The parallel ruts worn in the carpet from her maneuvering from the living room to the kitchen and the formidable musculature of her arms. Her legs, hidden within dark-dyed jeans, are in comparison a pair of withered saplings, her upper body compensating in that same way a creature in nature adapts to its circumstances. Bats use sonar to fly at night. Cats, like my pretend missing feline, Thor, use their whiskers to negotiate tight spaces.

Marie Rader uses her arms and shoulders to get around.

I wonder if her heart and conscience have adapted so that she can ignore her husband's serial killing. Or if she even has an inkling of the kind of man she married?

My survival adaptive behavior is my ability to look into another's eye and flat out lie. No pulse increase. No looking away to the left. Just as bald faced as I can be.

I do it in her kitchen while she prepares the ice tea.

"Can I use your restroom?" I ask.

She looks in my direction and smiles.

"Certainly." She points with that muscled arm of hers. "Down the hall by the bedrooms."

I disappear and start soaking in everything I can as I make my way toward the bathroom. I look for any sign that my mother might have been brought here. I look out the window and see that the yard has an enormous pond, a former swimming pool, and I wonder if there is a trapdoor leading to a space under it. There is but a single photograph on the wall by the window of Mr. and Mrs. Rader, as they stand—or rather he stands—side by side at their wedding. The photo is of poor quality and I only hold it in my sights long enough to see if there is any similarity in his appearance and my own.

I let out a puff of air. Good. *There isn't.* But when I study his face a little closer, I see something very familiar in it. I can't place it though, and I don't have time to process this right now.

Glancing back the way I came, I am glad to see Marie is out of sight, still fixing the drinks, and I hurry down the hall and twist a doorknob. It's a bedroom. I scan it and it appears to be a guest room with a single bed and a dried floral arrangement on a nightstand. It also appears as if it has seldom, if ever, been used.

Of course not. They have no children.

Or at least Mrs. Rader hasn't had any.

The next room along, the master bedroom, has two beds. I can tell which one is his and which is hers. The same parallel ruts join the furthest bed near the headboard. It looks so sad, so nothing.

I tread softly back to the bathroom I am supposed to be using, emerging from it a few moments later to find Marie literally parked by the door.

Got to admit, what she might know scares the life out of me, but I don't show it. I smile weakly instead.

"Are you all right?" she asks.

I pat my stomach. "I'm fine. Just something I ate."

She nods and I follow her back to the kitchen where she's set two glasses of ice tea. I'm touched by her kindness. A lemon slice slinks into the bottom of each glass like a descending moon.

"Sweet tea," she says.

My pulse is racing after that mini tour of the house. My stomach actually *is* upset now. I don't know if I should tell Marie what I know or call the police. I decide neither is a good idea. I don't trust the police. Alex Rader *is* the police. Marie Rader is trapped in a wheelchair, and I'm afraid if I tell her the truth she'll have a heart attack or something. Instead, as I figure out what to do, we talk about my missing cat. We talk about her water feature, a swimming pool that apparently made no sense for a paraplegic, but suited her love of koi. She talks about her fine needlework. She tells me that she and her husband own property out in Issaquah. That piques my interest, but when I try to ferret out a few details I feel a wave of nausea flow through me. I shouldn't have said that something I ate for lunch has made me ill. I just made one of my lies a truth.

"I need to use your restroom again," I say, setting down the glass, but missing the table. I see it fall to the floor and shatter.

Then nothing.

Blackness drapes over me.

Chapter Sixteen

Cash: None.
Food: None.
Shelter: None.
Weapons: None.
Plan: Stay alive.

I OPEN MY EYES BUT I can't see. I want to feel around, but I can't move my arms and nothing touches my chewed-nail fingertips. I feel a vibration under my back, a kind of rumbling. I feel motion. I have no idea what happened. I play the last moments before everything went black. The lady watering her hanging flower basket. My "missing" cat. The wheelchair. The ice tea.

I'm in a moving car, I think. Whose car?

Turning my head to the side, I see that the space is larger. *A van.* I'm in *the* van that was in the Raders' garage. There are no windows, but I notice a sliver of faint light at my feet. The door. The way out. I twist as much as possible but it is of no use. My body is a stiff board.

Maybe I am dead.

I take a deep breath and know that I'm alive. I'm also in trouble. Serious trouble. I refuse to panic. I try rocking my body, but I am too weak to do anything. When I try to use my hands to push myself upward, I feel the resistance of tape or ropes that have bound me into a cocoon.

Behind me I hear a radio.

The van stops. It lurches. It slows. I feel the sensation of running over a gravel road. I hear the wheels go over a roadway with loose, jagged stone.

Then it stops.

The door on the driver's side opens. Shuts. The crunching of gravel.

And although it is dark outside, I see things very clearly when the back door slides open. In the moonlight, a face.

I know that face.

My father.

Next to me is Marie's wheelchair.

Then his hand reaches for me. It comes for my face like a spear does in some 3D movie. I try to turn away and I scream for him to stop. Then just as blackness comes once more, I hear Marie's voice. Only this time it isn't soothing and sweet. It isn't all kittens and rainbows and water features. There's a hard edge to it. Also, for the very first time, I hear his voice. For a monster's voice, it is kind of high pitched.

"I want her and her mother erased," Marie says. "Your obsession ends now."

"Or you'll do what, Marie?" he says, barely challenging her.

"I'll make you pay."

"I've already paid a lifetime over and over by staying with

you."

"You could have left anytime."

"I couldn't."

"Just get it over with."

I WAKE UP IN A windowless chamber, the humming sounds of a generator and a string of light bulbs glowing above me.

Someone is stroking my hair, and for a second I wonder if I am in a dream. But then I hear her voice.

"Honey," says my mother.

I'm cradled in her lap like I used to be when we watched crime TV shows together—a long time ago, when I was small. She continues to stroke my dyed and cut hair.

My first words are not tender or concerned. Ever since I found out the truth, the lies she told me have lined the back of my mind. I can't just pretend that now that I have found her everything is OK. I'm glad to see her—see her *alive*—more than anything. But I'll get to that.

"Why did you lie to me?" I ask.

Mom is dirty and her hair is a mess. Her eyes are swimming in tears and she leans close.

"I'm sorry," she says. "But you were too young to understand the truth."

"I'm sixteen."

"Now . . . but you were a kid, Rylee. You were my baby. I wanted to protect you." She closes her eyes for a second, trying to compose herself, then asks, "Where is Hayden?"

I open my mouth to reply, but I don't know how freely I can speak and I indicate so by darting my eyes around the space we're in, which I assume to be a mine or a cave. "He's gone," she whispers, meaning my rapist father. "He'll be back tomorrow."

"Hayden's with Aunt Ginger," I tell her, still keeping my voice as low as I can. The hum of the generator probably provides some cover for our words, but I don't trust my mother's judgement anymore. I love her. I kind of hate her too. I want to ask her a zillion questions but only one seems to matter.

"Is there a way out of here?"

Mom strokes my hair some more. She doesn't say anything for what seems like a very long time so I already know the answer. She knows that I do.

"There's only one way out and that's the way in," she says.

I shift my weight and stand. I look to the door she's indicating. It's a big steel plate, rusted by the damp air. As I look around, I notice that we aren't in a mine, at least not like the ones I've read about. This isn't a coal seam. A gold or silver mine. We're surrounded by the undulating form of metamorphic rock. Granite. We're in a quarry and it's a good bet that it's the one in Issaquah near where Leanne Delmont's body was found.

Leaving her there was a taunt. An FU to his fellow law enforcement officials. I am so going to kill him when I get the chance. And when I do, I'm going to enjoy every moment of it. But with none of my weapons and the plan that would go with each, I'm unsure how any of this will go down.

"I'm sorry," Mom repeats.

"It's okay. It's not your fault." When I say that I mean it wasn't her fault that she was abducted and raped and tortured. Not at all. But she holds some blame for my stepfather's death and the life we've lived.

"Why didn't you just call the police on him?" I ask, knowing the answer from Aunt Ginger, but still wanting to hear it from her lips.

"He *was* the police,' she says. And then she looks at me and starts her side of the story.

COURTNEY SAT IN HER CAR *in front of her parents' house, just outside of the Tacoma city limits. She turned off the ignition and watched as a vehicle crawled behind her. It had been four months since she'd reported her abduction. She was no longer at a regular high school, but attended an alternative school. Most of the kids enrolled were branded creative rebels but that's not why she was there. Her issues were deep. Counselling eased some of the burden of what she'd been through. But not all of it. She revisited that place where she was held captive every night when she closed her eyes.*

The car parked in the space next to hers.

The sight of him stunned and silenced her when all her mouth wanted to do was let out a scream. She swung the car door open and started to move as quickly as she could toward the front door of the house.

"Stop! Courtney!"

His voice was a command.

She turned to look at him and opened her mouth to scream but he was already on her with his hand over it.

His hot breath pulsed on her ear. "Say a word and I'll kill your sister. Your parents too."

She relaxed, not because she trusted him, but because she knew that fighting him would only give him more pleasure. That resistance and pain only brought him relief.

Even joy.

He caught her full attention and his fingertips slid downward to the gun clipped to his waistband. Previously, his weapons against her had been ropes, wires, and his body.

"I know what you are," she said, her voice meek, subservient—and she hated that as much as she loathed him.

He touched her cheek and she stood there, frozen in fear.

"I know what you are," he said. "You're mine. I've marked you. You belong to me now."

He was talking about the tattoo, and she reached for her shoulder. She had never shown it to anyone. Not Ginger. Not her folks. By ignoring it and never looking at it when she showered or changed clothes, she willed the tattoo, and the ordeal, away.

But she couldn't right then. He was looking at her with those grotesque eyes. They penetrated. They degraded. They reminded her of what she had done to stay alive and how she got away. But mostly they were a reminder that he was out there. Hunting. Killing, probably.

"I could have killed you when I had you. I picked you on purpose. You were the perfect victim. Couldn't have been better. The others were collateral. I saw your file. I knew your past. I knew that you were a liar and that no one would ever believe you. I can kill you right now."

"Then do it," she said.

He shook his head. "Not here. Not now. I'll kill your sister first."

She wanted to defy him and she tried with a threat. "I will scream right now. Someone will come. I'll tell them everything."

"You already have," he said, laughing. "No one believed you

the first time. It's the definition of mental illness . . . doing the same thing again and again and expecting a different outcome." He paused and watched her. "Are you crazy, Courtney? If you are, I don't mind. I like crazy."

"I will tell," she sputtered out.

He shrugged. He knew the threat was an idle one.

"My word against yours. And if you make me mad, Ginger dies."

She'd never said her sister's name to him. Not once. Not when she'd cried in the darkness for help. Not a single time. But he knew Ginger's name.

She took a step backwards from the driveway to the lawn. Her heel caught on the rubber landscape-edging and she fell, landing flat on her back. She was wearing a chambray fabric dress, thin and loose.

He frowned. "You're . . . " He bent down, his eyes on the already noticeable bump of her abdomen, and his eyes brightened. "Courtney. You have something for me?"

"Nothing," she said, recoiling under his scrutiny. "Nothing for you."

He smiled. His teeth shone white in the early evening and she remembered how he'd used them on her body; how he'd defiled her with his mouth while she was tied up, helpless, screaming in that quarry cavern that he'd turned into a kind of deranged bachelor pad. It had a bed. A lamp. It had a box of ropes, knives, needles, ink and wire.

"Let's see what's in my toy box today," he'd told her the first night he'd taken her.

Courtney stood up, shivering on the cold, damp grass.

"I promise I won't make trouble," she said. "Just leave me alone.

I will never tell again. Just go."

She didn't want to mention the baby. If he was uncertain at all, she was not going to confirm her condition. When the baby was born, she told herself, she'd give it up for adoption, to an agency with the strictest confidentiality policy.

A smile came to the monster's lips and it took everything Courtney had to hold the contents of her stomach inside. She wanted to scream. She wanted to vomit. But she didn't, of course. Because though she thought she could never love her baby, she knew that someone else could.

And that someone else would never be her abductor.

Her rapist.

Her baby's father.

My father.

I SIT IN SILENCE AS my mother pauses and more jagged pieces of the ragged puzzle that was our life until barely a week ago fall into place. I am still mad at her, but I find myself clinging to her, comforting her. There is so much to know and if these are to be our last hours together then I need to show her love.

"How long before he comes back?" I ask, looking toward the steel door that holds us captive in this dark, scary place.

"Tomorrow. When you were unconscious and he brought you in here he said he'd be back tomorrow. He left some sandwiches and some ice tea."

"Don't drink the ice tea," I say, urgency rising in my voice. "Marie made it."

"Who's Marie?" Mom asks, obviously confused.

"You don't know about Marie?"

She shakes her head.

"His wife," I say. "Alex Rader's wife, Marie. I trusted her because she was in a wheelchair."

A look overtakes my mother's face. It is the kind of reaction that a kid makes when he looks up from a really hard math problem. The look that says something puzzling has finally been figured out.

Chapter Seventeen

Cash: None.
Food: Two tunafish sandwiches.
Shelter: Cave.
Weapons: Rocks.
Plan: Get ready.

THE WOMAN IN THE WHEELCHAIR was struggling to get it up over the curb.

Courtney had missed the bus at school and was making the long walk home. While waiting at the crosswalk for the light to change, she couldn't help but notice the young woman in the wheelchair trying to get wherever she was going to.

"Do you need a hand?" she asked.

The woman looked over her shoulder and nodded. She is blond, pretty and only a few years older than Courtney.

As Courtney got closer the woman in the chair started to cry.

"This just isn't right," she said.

"Let me help you."

The moment was awkward because the woman wouldn't—or couldn't—stop crying.

"I never should have imagined I could manage out here on my own," she said between sobs. "It's too hard. All of this."

"I'm sorry," Courtney said. She thought a moment and said something truthful and to the point. "Look, I don't even know what to say here. I don't know if I should say you'll be all right or that you'll get there or what? All I can think of is that I'm sorry."

The woman looked up at her.

"I appreciate that," she said. "I've been in this chair for a while now and I'm still getting used to it. Sometimes I just need a little push."

"I can do that," Courtney said, gripping the back of the chair.

"My car's over there." The woman indicated the far reaches of the parking lot. "I guess I can manage now."

Courtney didn't stop. She didn't need to hurry home, and doing something nice for someone else was a big part of who she was.

"That's all right," she said and the wheels glided over the asphalt toward a bronze-colored van parked by the dumpsters. "I don't mind at all."

For the rest of their time together, neither one said much more. Courtney had already exhausted any commentary about the weather and she certainly wasn't about to bring up anything about the circumstances that led this young woman to being chair-bound.

When she'd arranged the wheelchair next to the van, the woman instructed Courtney to go to the rear of the vehicle.

"I have a lift in the back," she said.

Courtney nodded and, as she turned, a hand reached from behind and put something over her face.

Then nothing. Just black. Just the beginning of a nightmare that would haunt her for her entire life, a nightmare that would *make her give up everything she had. Her family. Her beloved sister. Her home. Her name. Everything would be gone. She would not be a doctor, like she'd hoped to be. She would not be anything but a figure among the shadows. She'd give up everything except her daughter.*

That was one thing she could never do.

AS I LIE THERE IN the semidarkness with Mom, hearing her story, learning what it was that transformed her life, I want to know what awaits us. I want to ask her what exactly he did to her, as if there could be something worse than the rape that made me. I want to ask her why she decided to keep me, but I already know that. It is the same reason that propelled me to find her. My stepfather, my brother, neither of them had endured what we had those first years alone on the run. Hayden never knew any other life. Rolland loved Mom enough to try to save her. Hayden's reality had never shifted. Rolland never wanted anything other than to protect Mom.

But we both had known another life. My mom, definitely. Me, a sliver of one. We didn't start to run until around my fourth birthday. I know from talking to Aunt Ginger that a play had been made for me at the hospital the day I was born. I understand that Alex Rader wanted a piece of me. Yet, we didn't run straight away.

"What happened to us?" I ask, an opening question that could lead to a torrent of responses. I want a response to something specific, but casting a wide net might get me something I don't expect.

Maybe even something I don't really want to know.

Her blue eyes lock on mine. She knows that her subterfuge hurt me and in her hesitation I see an opportunity to force her hand.

"I love you, Mom," I say. "But you should have trusted me. I always trusted you."

"That isn't fair," she says. "You were a child. Any mother would have done the same thing."

"Maybe, but what also isn't fair is that I've never had a real friend in my life. I've never stayed overnight at any other girl's house. I've never had a birthday party that included anyone but you. Then later, Rolland and Hayden. I never once knew what it was like to confide in someone other than you."

She looks away into the darkness.

I add more. "I never knew that I had an aunt named Ginger, but you did. You saw her as recently as Labor Day weekend last year. Don't get me wrong. I love you. But you don't have the right to tell me anything isn't fair. Not ever again as long as we live. Which might not be much longer anyway."

Tears stream down Mom's face, but I don't offer her any comfort this time. In a very real way, I feel better right now than I ever have. She might have done all that she did for the right reasons, but right reasons don't necessarily mean the results were any good.

"I don't even know when my real birthday is because you've switched it up so many times."

"March seventeenth," she says. "You're sixteen."

I'm way past really caring about that right now. I'm thinking of Hayden, Aunt Ginger and even Caleb, and worrying if I'll ever see them again.

"What happened to Bill Walters? What happened to the hero you've told me all these years was my biological father?"

Now she's really crying. I don't comfort her. Not really. I've been through a lot the past few days. I know she has too, but part of me knows that the mystery of my life and how we lived will never be fully known to me. There isn't enough time for that. I'm looking for broad brushstrokes now. I'll dig in deeper, if I survive.

If *we* survive.

"Bill Walters never existed in your life. That's why you have no memory of him."

"But we had his picture on the TV in Minneapolis before we moved to wherever we lived next."

"Iowa," she says.

"Whatever," I snap back. "That's not the point. The point is that you let me believe my dad was a war hero. You told me that Bill Walters was my dad. Do you know that I used to take his photograph into my room at night and put it under my pillow?"

"Of course. I'm the one who moved it back to the TV in the morning, Rylee."

I want to shut her down a little by telling her that I hate that particular name and that I'm mad that she always got prettier names when we moved. But I don't. I know that would be petty and there will be time for that later. At least I hope so.

"Who was he?" I ask. "I had his photo. The dog tags?"

"He was Ginger's husband. I got the photo and the tags from her. She gave me everything I needed to get out of Tacoma and start over."

Aunt Ginger? Her husband?

The tags. The photograph.

Props.

Just like my cat flyer.

"I thought they were divorced," I say. "I didn't see his picture at her place. Just a bunch of us." I glower a little in the dimming light.

The generator is sputtering.

Before Mom answers, I turn to a more practical subject.

"Are we losing power?"

She nods. "Yes. It will be dark in a few minutes. Let's go over to the pen."

"The pen?" I ask, the term making my skin crawl.

"That's what Alex calls the spot where we sleep."

"You're on a first name basis?"

"I do what I have to. I got out of a place like this once. I intend to do it again."

"We need to find a way out of here now," I say. "That's what we need to do. We don't need to go to the pen."

I get up and scan the walls, but they are solid granite. We're trapped inside a mountain. My impulse is to scream for help but I know by the pressure on my ears that we are down deep. Soon we will be in the dark. And then he will come back. There will be nothing but blackness in between.

"How did you get out that first time?"

The generator is rumbling louder. Then it coughs to a stop. The place is dark and silent. Mom doesn't say anything and I can't hear her breathe.

"Mom?"

189

A hand reaches for me and I pull away even though my brain tells me she's the only one here. Her hand swipes for me once more and I let her catch me. She takes my hand and we inch across the gravel floor toward the pen. Mom is crying. I can't hear her, but I can feel the tremble and shudder of her silent tears.

"How did you get out?" I repeat as she pulls me onto what feels like a mattress. It is itchy and smelly and I'll never complain about the Best Western again. Her arms wrap around me and we sit there in the dark.

Silence. What's the matter with her? She needs to pull herself together. Now.

I'm inches from her face, but I shout.

"Talk to me, Mom!"

Warm air leaks from her lips and she finally speaks.

"Leanne," she says. "Leanne got me out."

Chapter Eighteen

Cash: None.
Food: One tunafish sandwich.
Shelter: Underground.
Weapons: Rocks.
Plan: Whatever it takes. Whatever it is.

WHEN SHE FINALLY STOPS WEEPING, Mom tells me about the pen and how it was different when Alex Rader brought her to a similar place when she was sixteen. There was no generator, for one thing. There was also a partition dividing the space into two. It was so dark that the first day, after he had raped her and left her bound and gagged, it took her a while to feel the presence of another person.

"I thought I was alone," she says, unspooling the words slowly. "I thought that there was no way that what he was doing to me could be done to another human being. When I woke up I was sore in every place you could imagine, and one place that I didn't expect. My shoulder. I thought that maybe I'd been injured when I tried to fight him off."

"The tattoo," I say.

She doesn't answer, but I imagine that she nods. Maybe she is even a little proud of me for figuring out that she and the other girls had tattoos.

"There was no generator noise then. Just the dripping of a drainage pipe and the sound of someone whimpering through the partition. Alex was gone and I called over toward the noise. A moment later, there was an answer."

"MY NAME IS LEANNE. HE'S going to kill us. I think he already killed a girl. He put me in her clothes."

Courtney felt her own heart heaving in her aching chest.

"My name is Courtney," she said. "How long have you been here?"

The girl was crying. "I don't know. The days all run together. I want to go home. I don't want to do this."

Courtney didn't either.

"Are you tied up? Can you get free? He has me pinned down here."

"Duct tape. He took it from over here when he brought you in."

Courtney twisted her wrists until she felt the tape's adhesive backing pull small hairs from her arms.

"Yes, he's taped my wrists," she called back, her voice raw from her screams. "I think he's taped my ankles too. I can't lift my head up to see. I'm pinned down."

Like a frog in Biology. Pinned. Waiting for the tip of the scalpel and the intrusion of steel into its fragile body. Her fragile body. He wasn't going to cut her. But he was going to violate her over and over until there was nothing left of her. Her spirit, her body. All vanquished by his twisted desire.

"He used a rope on me," Leanne said. "I think I can get off this mattress and make it to you. Maybe we can help each other get out of here. I don't want to die."

"We're not going to die," Courtney said, not knowing if that was true.

Leanne Delmont, just sixteen, slithered across the dirt of the floor like an injured animal. In the dimmest of light, her eyes were wide and full of panic. She inched herself up to Courtney's side and tried to assess the situation.

Their eyes met.

"Yes, he taped you," she says as she immediately and frantically tried to work the tape loose with her hands, which were bound by a nylon cord. She had more freedom of motion than *Alex Rader's* newest captive, Courtney, and she gave it everything she had.

"I don't know," she said as she struggled with the tape, her words choked with fear. "I can't get it. It's too tight."

Courtney yelped into the semi-darkness.

"I'm hurting you," Leanne said, slowing a little, but still trying to find a way to undo or tear off the silvery duct tape. It was worse than trying to find the end of a roll of plastic wrap, a mundane thought that came to her in the midst of the horror at hand.

Whatever pain Leanne thought she was inflicting was nothing compared with the ordeal Courtney had experienced with Alex Rader when he punched her in the face and threw himself on top of her, ripping her clothes, her body, with the force of a maniac.

"It doesn't hurt," Courtney lied. "Keep going."

Leanne was in a frenzy as she worked the tape with her fingertips, and then somehow managed to lean in and bite the binding with her teeth. Hot tears fell over Courtney, but she didn't say another *word. Leanne kept going until Courtney's hands were free.*

In a flash, Courtney righted herself, quickly undoing the tape around her ankles.

She was free.

"Help me," Leanne said.

Courtney turned her attention to Leanne and began to struggle with the tightly-bound ropes that tied her wrists and her feet.

"Who is he?"

"A cop," *said Leanne.* "He told me he was a police officer and that my parents had been in a terrible accident. I got in his car. I was so stupid. I didn't think to ask him how he found me. Or how he knew my name. That was so stupid. He showed me his badge."

Leanne had been beaten, raped, and humiliated in every way by a monster, yet she blamed herself.

"It isn't your fault," *Courtney said, as she managed to undo the binding ensnaring Leanne's wrists. They were raw and bleeding and, for a second, until blood covered the gouges made by the rope, she thought she saw Leanne's wrist bone.*

"He sat me in the front, the passenger seat. When the seatbelt didn't work he told me that it was a little tricky and he reached over to help me. Then his hand went over my face. And then it went black."

The sole source of light in the dark space was a battery-powered lantern. Courtney hurled herself toward it. She held the lantern in the air, noticing for the first time that Leanne was completely naked, bloodied and bruised.

They had to get out.

Now.

"The only way out of here is through the door," *Leanne said.*

AS MOM TELLS THE STORY that I suspect she's never told anyone before, I see her in new way. I already know that she is strong. I've never doubted that. I know that she loves me and Hayden with every fibre of her being. I know by the way she can barely say Rolland's name—any of his names—that she is beyond heartbroken that he's gone.

Because she loved him.

Us.

Me.

What I didn't know until this moment is that what happened to Leanne Delmont haunts my mother's every waking moment. I never knew about Leanne, of course. Yet, it seems that she was always there with Mom. I wonder how often we'd been sitting together while Leanne's face came to my mother's mind. Had it been during a scary movie when the boogieman rushes toward a screaming girl with a roaring chainsaw? Had it been at Christmas when she undid the twine and ribbons of a package that had been wrapped just for her?

Did duct tape at the hardware store take her back to a Leanne memory?

I suspect all those things are possible. And more. More than I can imagine because until that moment I had no idea the role Leanne Delmont played in Mom's survival.

And my own.

The words come out in a cough at first. Like she's choking them out of someplace dark and deep in her memory. Each word is coated in a strange combination of regret and appreciation for the girl who posed so prettily on the log on the beach at Point Defiance.

She tells me how she and Leanne waited in the darkness for hours for Alex Rader to return. Some of the emotion has left her now. As she resumes her story, she somehow switches her tone to a detached, almost rote, manner, which I know is for my benefit. Her way of checking herself is to ensure that the reality of what transpired is communicated to me, but is done so in a way that maintains some distance. I don't tell her that I met the families of the girls and how the tragedy of losing their daughters has changed their lives forever. She knows that. It has changed my life too.

"We made a pact," she says. "We knew there were two of us and one of him, but Leanne was physically weak. She'd been there for days and she . . . "

Mom stops for a beat and I squeeze her hand. I need to know exactly what they did. I need to figure out how the hell we're going to get out of here. I already know that Leanne didn't make it, but I don't know why and I don't know how she really died.

"She was exhausted," I say.

"Yes. Weakened by what he did. Tired. Hungry. She was scared as hell that she didn't have the strength to overpower him. I told her that she did. I promised that we'd get out. Together. Rylee, it was a lie. It was a terrible, terrible lie. Seeing her injuries, I just didn't . . . I didn't think she could make it."

"I know you wanted her to survive, Mom," I say.

She cries and I ask her to continue. I'm gentle in my request. But I'm also more pragmatic. I must know. I need to get us out of here. I'm stronger than she is. And I'm not leaving her behind.

"What was the plan?" I ask as she stops for a moment and

we both listen to the nothingness of the prison in which we are held by the monster that is my father.

I will kill him in part for what he did to my mother, but also for what he did to Leanne. I expect Shannon and Megan faced the same fate in the darkness, but I don't know for sure. I only know what I'm hearing from my mom.

The victim who got away.

"We knew he'd go to her first," she continues. "She'd been there longer and she was certain of his routine. He'd change out the battery, unzip his pants and begin by saying the ugliest things a man can say to a girl."

I am grateful that she doesn't repeat those things now. I don't want disgust and anger in the way of my rage.

"We found one rock," she says, stopping again to listen, as if he is coming. Or maybe in her mind right now she is remembering the sound of his footsteps on the crushed rock outside the door.

"The rock we found was the only one that was large enough to do the job, but small enough that I could lift it. And we waited."

Now Mom starts to cry again. She's dehydrated because I told her not to drink the ice tea and I wonder how she can even manage to expel another tear.

"This part is really hard," she says. "It's really hard, Rylee."

"I know," I answer.

But I really don't.

"We knew he would abuse her first. Then he'd come to me. I bound her wrists again."

She stops. Takes a breath.

"Go on, Mom," I say, softly but with conviction. "We have to get out of here."

She nods.

"I bound her wrists. She did her best to help me appear as though I was still taped up, by putting the old, broken duct tape around my wrists and ankles. We, Rylee, we . . . we got back on our mattresses and waited. I had the stone. Leanne told me to wait until he was on top of her. Abusing her. Stealing every bit of life from her. She told me to count to one hundred . . . have you ever counted to one hundred in your head? Have you ever counted to one hundred when a man is raping a girl next to you and you are free enough to try to stop it?"

She knew I hadn't. Her tears are a silent torrent now. I hold her and she finishes what happened next.

"When I got to about fifty I couldn't take it. She'd been crying and screaming out and he was telling her over and over that she was a worthless piece of garbage and that no man would ever want her. That her life was pointless and she lived only to serve him. I got up and crawled as quietly as I could and struck him as hard as I could on the head with the stone. He fell on top of her. I thought I had killed him. I pushed him off and tugged at Leanne. She'd been badly beaten again. I pulled the key from his pocket and we started for the door."

Mom stops and looks over at the door.

"That door. That one."

I nod and hold her tighter. She whispers the rest of what happened in my ear as though saying it any louder will make it more concrete, more real than it already is.

"She was right behind me," Mom says. "I unlocked the door

and we started out. We were both crying and . . . when I turned around, Leanne wasn't there. Alex had grabbed her by the ankle and tackled her. He yelled at me to come back and I started to. I needed to get Leanne away from him. But she screamed at me to keep going. All of a sudden she stopped screaming. I thought he'd killed her. He called to me that he'd kill me, my parents, and my sister."

The next question I ask is not meant to hurt her. She's been through all of that. I cannot believe that my mother left Leanne behind.

"Do you blame yourself?" I ask.

I know I would never have left Leanne.

She takes a breath and speaks without a whisper this time.

"Every moment of the day," she says.

Good, I think. I want to turn her rage about what Alex Rader has done into something useful.

"Then let's finish what you tried to do. For Leanne, Shannon, Megan, and for us, Mom. Let's make sure he's dead this time."

AS WE GO TO SLEEP in the darkness Hayden comes to mind. I wonder how he's doing and if he's worried. I think about Caleb too and I imagine that he's at school, though I don't know what time of day it is. Everything is black. I think about Leanne's mother in that big house overlooking the bay and how I want her to know that Leanne sacrificed herself to save my mom. That I'm grateful and sorry at the same time. I want Mrs. Delmont to know that if she had ever thought her daughter was selfish and self-absorbed she was wrong. When the moment of truth came, Leanne chose to help someone else.

199

Her spirit is with me right now.

Help someone else. Someone who needs it. I think of Selma at the rest stop. I remember her face. The license plate. I don't know that she's in trouble. But I wish now that I'd been more like Leanne when I had the chance, and found out for sure if anything was wrong. As strong as I think I am, I was weak at a time when I should have shown fortitude. I vow that I never will be that person again.

My mother and I are wrapped around each other and her heartbeat and breathing bring me comfort. I move my hand over the smelly mattress and I hit something sharp. I don't cry out, but it hurts like hell.

Instead, I smile.

I've got a weapon after all.

Chapter Nineteen

Cash: None.
Food: None.
Shelter: Cave.
Weapons: Rocks, bedspring.
Plan: Kill the MF.

THE GENERATOR KICKS ON AND we know that he's back. My father enters our prison with a gun pointed at me. I recognize it as my gun. I know this is his idea of taunting me, showing me his superiority.

"Daddy's home," he says.

"Leave her alone," Mom tells him as she pulls her arm tighter around my shoulder.

"Courtney, honey. You must not think much of me," he says. "I'd never rape my own daughter. Not now that I've found her."

I want to laugh out loud. He thinks he's funny, ironic. I know he's a pig, a scumbag. Worse than anything I'd scrape off my shoe.

"I found *you*," I finally say. "It wasn't hard."

"I wasn't the one in hiding," he says. "I never have been."

He emerges from the shadows. I see his face properly for the first time. I keep my emotions in check, but I am completely stunned.

He looks exactly like my brother.

I catch Mom's gaze and she telegraphs to me what I think I know.

Alex Rader has found us at least once before in my lifetime.

I am reminded of the time we talked about the members of the Donner Party, a group of pioneers who'd been trapped in the Sierra Nevada Mountains during a blizzard and how they'd resorted to cannibalism in order to survive.

"You can't imagine what people will do to survive."

"Cannibalism? That's gross," I said.

"I've done worse," Mom answered.

Something told me back then not to ask what was worse than eating another person. I really didn't want to know.

Now I know.

MY FATHER LOOKS AT ME. He is so average that I would not ever have picked him out as a creeper or anything. He's got sandy hair that is thinning slightly at the temples. His eyes are like Hayden's. His hands, gripping the gun, are slender, like mine.

"The police will find you," I say.

"I am the police," he says, pointing the gun at Mom. "I'm also the judge."

And the executioner too.

"Let her go," Mom says.

"Not happening. We're a family, Courtney."

"We're not," she shouts back.

It's a tit-for-tat kind of exchange that I know won't get us anywhere. I know Mom has had the conversation with him before and that he has a hold on her in a way that I can't fully understand.

Is it guilt over Leanne?

"What do you want from me?" I ask, inserting myself into the conversation.

The air in the space around us is still enough that I can feel his breath even at a distance. I don't want to be any closer, but I doubt I will have much say in that.

"Still deciding," he says.

"Please, Alex," Mom says. "I'll do anything you want me to do."

He looks at her with a leer. "You always do, babe."

His words are acid on my face.

You can't imagine what people will do to survive.

"I hate you, Mom," I say to her, my voice like ice. "You lied to me!"

Mom mutters something about being sorry, but I don't allow her to say anything else. I am about to put on the biggest hissy fit that the world has ever seen. I don't mean any of the words that spew from my lips, but I say them with such conviction I don't think my mother believes I'm faking anything.

She so doesn't know what I'm capable of. Whatever she did to survive was her choice. To run was to acknowledge that Alex Rader was more powerful than she. I'm not going to let him get away. I'm not going to let him live. I don't care—and this is the truth—if I'm the last one standing.

I go on. "You are as big a freak as this piece of shit here,"

I say, looking at my bio dad. His Hayden eyes blink. A smile curls on his lips. He's liking my rage. He likes a fighter. I'll give him one. I can be as cold as he can be. I can be just as ruthless.

"You're pathetic, Mom," I yell at her. "I don't know why I bothered to find you. You made my life a living hell. You took me away from everyone and everything I ever loved. I'm not even sure that I can love any more. I might not be any better than Psycho Dad."

That's the biggest lie I ever told. I do love Mom. I loved Rolland. I love Hayden. I even have feelings for Caleb that fall somewhere beyond that gray area between crush and love. I don't know.

But I'm not done with my phony recriminations. Not yet.

"To think I actually felt sorry for you. You dragged us around like we were nomads and I thought that you were running from an old boyfriend. Then I find out he's a goddamn serial killer and that you have been with him again. Hayden! Hayden's his little boy, isn't he?"

"He's not his," she says. Her eyes are blistering at me. "Don't say it!"

"I'll say whatever I goddamn want. You have no say any more how I live or what I do. Your days of scurrying around trying to avoid the light of truth are over. You make me sick. You have betrayed me and, honestly Mom, I'm so sick of every lie that spews out of your mouth. At least Fuckface Dad here is honest."

I'm pleased with that last line. I've never said the F word in front of Mom before. It felt a little liberating, which is ironic as we are both doomed by the man that killed at least four others.

"You left Leanne!" I continue ranting, while Mom just sits there like a stunned bump. "You are such a bitch!"

I'm pleased again with that line too and I stop. I evaluate. Dear old Serial Killer Dad looks like he's enjoying the tirade. He might even think he has an ally. I doubt he's going to rape me. Even for a serial killer that might be too low.

"I did it for you," Mom finally says.

"Bullshit," I shoot back. "You didn't even know you were pregnant with that asshole's baby when you left Leanne to die." I pause and go for the jugular. "You only thought to save yourself. That's what this whole thing is about. Isn't it, Mom?"

She's crying now. She's slumped on the edge of the makeshift bed and is sobbing like a baby. I hit her in the truth spot and I hit her hard. In a second, I'm on top of her trying to comfort her.

"I'm sorry, Mom. I'm scared. I didn't mean it."

Now her face is pressed against the mattress and I can't hear her response.

"You two knock it off," Alex says.

I turn to him. "She's a bitch, but she's my mom."

He comes closer and tugs me roughly by the shoulder, hurting me.

"She's my bitch," he says.

"And you're mine," I say, as I take the straightened coil from the mattress and shove it in his left eye. Hard as I can. He screams so loudly dust falls from the ceiling, but his pain only fuels me. I scream as loud as I can and I twist the heavy metal wire like a corkscrew and pull.

Alex Rader only has one eye now. The other is hanging from a thread. His hands go up to his face and the gun falls to the mattress. I don't even think. There isn't time for that. I grab the gun and before he can take half a breath, pin its barrel to his forehead.

He looks at me with his good eye. Blood gushes down his face and into his mouth. His hand looks like he's wearing a shiny red glove. As I get ready to do what I know I have to do, he speaks.

"Look what you've done. You've hurt me bad. You don't know shit about me," he says, his voice a low croak.

My hand shakes a little and I tighten the sore muscles in my aching shoulder. I press the gun harder against his forehead and he winces.

"I don't care to know," I say.

The truth is, part of me *would* like to know. Part of me would like to understand the toxic DNA that we both share. I've done things in the last few days that I didn't know I could do.

Didn't want to do.

"You think I'm a monster," he says, his voice croaking more. *Emotion? Self-pity? Or is it that he knows he's going to die?*

"But I'm only half of one," he goes on. "There's part of me that's sorry. I did what I had to do. I had no choice."

If I had any food in my stomach I would like to vomit on him just then. He is repulsive. A liar. A blamer. He is going to give me some kind of bogus reason why he murders and rapes young women. Something that indicates it isn't his fault. That his DNA was coiled around a virus. That his mother bottle-fed him. That his father whipped him with the buckle end of a belt.

None of that will explain the evil he's done.

There's really no way of explaining that kind of nasty.

"You didn't *have* to do anything," I say.

"Do it," Mom calls out from behind me. "Rylee, kill him!"

Her voice is pleading and demanding at the same time. She's counting on me. She wants me to fix what she couldn't.

"I'm sorry," he says. "Please help me."

He releases his hand and his eye drops lower, swinging like a pendulum.

"I need a doctor. I'm begging you. I'll do whatever you want me to do. I promise. I'm good at following orders. I just don't want to die."

I feel the shaking of the gun in my hand, but I know that it isn't my hand that's causing the vibration. It's *him*. That bloody aberration that is my biological father is quaking in fear.

When I release the trigger, in my head I'm thinking four words.

This is for Leanne.

He falls to the floor. Without hesitating a beat, I plunge myself on top of him. I can't stop. It's like I'm not even me—the me that I pretended to be all my life. I'm the girl that I really am.

I fire a shot into his chest.

This is for Shannon.

And finally, I go lower. I unzip his pants, pull down his pale blue boxers and expose his penis. I've never seen a grown man's penis in person before and wonder if this is the source of his rage. It's small, shriveled and pathetic.

I blow it off the face of the earth with two shots.

One for Megan and one for Mom.

Chapter Twenty

Cash: None.
Food: None.
Shelter: None.
Weapons: Two bullets, a gun, and my hands.
Plan: Finish the job.

MOM AND I ARE IN Alex Rader's car, a boring Toyota Camry. I'm driving as fast as I can down the gravel road from the place where he'd raped and killed everyone but us, heading toward the lights of the Interstate. Our hearts are in sync, pounding like a couple of tom-toms. It is dark outside. I'm unsure of where we are until I see the signs to the highway. We haven't said a word. Not about the fact that I'm driving without a license or the fact that I'd called my mother every name in the book. Not that I've just executed my monster of a biological father.

And then I see it.

Hanging on a thin silver wire from the review mirror. A picture.

I slam on the brakes and the car slides before it stops.

"Was it a deer? I didn't see it."

I turn and look at her. She is a stranger to me right now. This woman who I adored and still love with every bit of my being, is as much as a stranger to me as Alex Rader was until I did what had to be done.

Shot him.

Dead.

"What's this, Mom?" My fingers grasp the photograph and, still keeping it on the chain, I pull it closer for a better view. It's a girl with a long blond ponytail, carefully arranged over her shoulder. She's wearing a bright yellow top. There's a gap in her teeth. She is four years old.

Her name at the time was Sarah.

My name at the time.

"How in the hell did he get that?" I ask.

"I had to," she says, her tone bordering on hysterical. "I had no choice but to keep him informed. To keep him away, I kept him close."

I am so disgusted I want to kick her out of the car. But I don't. I put the gas to the pedal. I just keep going. It's as if the speed will erase her words into a blur.

"Mom, you're messed up," I say, turning to her as I drive. "You're so messed up you don't even know how much."

She starts to shake. "He wanted a picture. I thought by giving it to him he'd leave us alone. He said he just wanted a reminder."

She turns away and looks out the window. But I don't let her. I grab her shoulder and yank her toward me. The car swerves a little and my adrenaline pumps.

"Look at me when I'm talking to you," I say. My anger is real now, and completely, I think, justifiably uncontained. "A reminder of what?"

Her eyes are empty. She doesn't cry out. She doesn't try to pull me in with a sob story about what she did. She's done with that. And for that, I'm glad.

"Of you," she says.

I don't know her. I don't understand her.

I do not scream at her, but I doubt if I did anyone would blame me.

"What did you do?" I ask. "Send him newsletters about Hayden and me? Did you keep him abreast of my first tooth, when I started walking, my first period? Jesus, Mom! What in the hell?"

She looks at me and I deflect her attempt for pity and support by focusing my eyes on the road.

"He said he'd kill you."

Perfect.

"No, Mom," I say without holding back my disappointment. "He didn't. He said he'd kill *you*, isn't that right? That's why we ran?"

Mom is thrashed and fretful. She shakes her head. "No, Rylee, that's not true."

"Don't call me that," I say, again as coolly as I can. "Call me my real name. Not Sarah. Not Katie. Not Rylee. My real name, Mom? Call me that."

Tears roll from her eyes and she wipes them on her dirty sleeve.

A dog barks somewhere and it fills the silence between us.

"Alexandra," she finally says. "Your name is Alex."

This is a balled up fist in my stomach but I just take it. I don't want to believe it. But there it is. She said it. My name. Like the tattoo she tried to erase. The one the other girls had too. Marked. I was marked too.

Alexandra.

I shake my head. "Who would do that? Who would do that with their child? Naming her after a monster?"

Mom doesn't answer for the longest time.

"People do what they have to do, honey. To survive."

I don't respond. I don't care anymore. I reach over and pull the photograph off the chain. I roll down the window and let it fly. Away.

I'm so done.

I PULL UP TO THE SAME DENNY'S in Kent and I let out my mother. We haven't spoken a word to each other for the past forty minutes. I guess she tried, but there was nothing left to say.

At least not by me and not right now.

"Go inside and wait," I tell her. It's an order, not a request.

She unbuckles her seatbelt and opens the door.

"What are you going to do?" Her eyes are red and her skin is dirty and blotchy.

"Something you should have done, Mom."

She doesn't ask me what my plans are and I'm grateful for that. I'm still making it up as I go along. I know that flexibility and randomness are protectors of the hunted. Rolland always said so. Even in the madness of the switch I knew that tipping a hand to anyone could only result in failure.

"Be careful," she tells me.

I know she means it, but I'm still so sickened and mad I don't wish her the same. Instead, I throw the vehicle into reverse, back up, then drive away. I watch Mom fade in the mirror. She's closer than she appears just then, but she's still very far away. I know that she's always been far away.

FUCHSIA LADY APPEARS TO BE GONE, which is good. From the glovebox of the Camry I retrieve a garage door opener. I push the button and the door at 2424 Summer Hill snakes up its track. I park next to the van. It is old, bronze-colored, with the words *Sun Catcher Express* painted merrily on the side. A big sun winks from just over the S. It is grotesque and if I didn't have something very important to do, I'd grab a paint can from the workbench and splatter it. I'd tear up the seats. I'd rip out the wheelchair lift. I would do all of that and more so that it never would be used for what it has been.

By Alex and Marie Rader.

It passes through my mind that Aunt Ginger's car isn't there and that I'm going to be in big trouble for losing it. Then I scratch that thought. Where Alex Rader ditched my aunt's car is the least of my worries. If I'm in trouble for anything, losing a car is somewhere at the very bottom of the list.

And the list is getting longer by the minute.

The garage door rolls down behind me and I don't need to use the keys because the door leading into the house is unlocked.

"Baby," I hear Marie call out. "I'm in the kitchen. Made you a pie today. Bet you'd love a slice."

I'd love to slice her.

I have the gun and the two bullets, but something tells me

that's going to be my last resort.

"Hi Marie," I say.

She's sitting in her chair, of course, at the kitchen table. In front of her is a cherry pie that looks like something out of a cooking magazine. Besides luring girls to their deaths, it seems that Marie Rader is a supremely talented baker. I love pie. In fact, cherry has long been my favorite. After I get done here, however, I know that the tart taste of the fruit will always make me think of her.

"Where's my husband?" she says, looking past me like I was a kitten that he'd dragged home and let loose to find his precious Marie.

"Alex?" I say casually, smiling. "He's dead, Marie."

Her head jerks, and I see a faint layer of sweat above her top lip.

"Lying little bitch," she snarls, scanning the table for something.

The knife.

I let her get it. I want to fight her. I want to feel her struggle and gasp. I want her to know how the others felt when their final moments came. The sequence of events that Marie, poor old wheelchair-bound Marie, set in motion with her pathetic but effective ruse of needing help.

I picture each one of Alex Rader's Sweet Sixteens—Leanne, Megan, Shannon, Mom, even me. I know that if not for Marie, all of those innocent girls would be alive. She'd been bait. And she'd gone along with it all.

"I shot him," I say without feeling. "In the head. In the crotch. Though neither of those areas were any use to you,

you withered bitch."

She doesn't blink. I wonder if her lids are paralyzed like her legs and her unfeeling heart.

"You're lying," she says, holding the knife.

Marie Rader doesn't even look human to me anymore. I think of her as a vile spider, scooting around with those arms of hers. I point the gun at her.

"Drop it."

"Make me," she says.

"Don't make it easy on me, Marie," I say.

She pushes back from the kitchen table, her arms rippling with sinew and muscle. I don't mind the challenge. I welcome it. I am consumed with fury, but I don't show it. It's like the idea of killing her is a drug to me. Like vanquishing her pathetic kind of evil will give me the biggest rush of my life. Bigger than shooting Alex. He was an obvious monster. I'm all but certain that I'll get so much more pleasure at taking out this insidious creature who has just baked the most beautiful pie I've ever seen.

"Why do you want to kill me?" she asks, inching closer. She's about to play the victim card. I can smell it. "My husband forced me to do all sorts of things," she goes on, blinking hard to force out a tear of emotion.

As if.

"Marie," I say. "You are like a Venus flytrap. So pure and tragic in your wheelchair, with no feeling below the waist. The truth is, you just sat there consumed with bitterness, waiting for the next girl to come by so you could entrap her."

"It wasn't like that, Rylee."

"You know my real name, don't you?"

She glances at the knife she's holding. Her face is hard again. I can tell she hates me for reminding her.

For knowing what I know. Not about him. But about how pathetic she is.

"Yes, I do," she says, her voice snapping a little. "I should have killed you when I had the chance, Alexandra. I should have tattooed you like the others and then slit your little throat. I know what you are to him."

It figures that she was the tattoo artist. The tail of a koi fish peeks out from under the bulging upper sleeve of her light pink T-shirt.

Just then, she starts coming toward me. She is turning the wheels of her chair with one arm. In her hand is the knife. I fire but miss. *Shit!* I have only one bullet left. I fire again, striking her in the kneecap. As if that would give me any hope for retreat. Blood flows from her dead limb and she doesn't even acknowledge it.

She can't feel anything.

The wheels of the chair spin faster.

I take a step back, thinking what to do. How I will stop her. I have no bullets. I drop the gun to the floor, regretting doing so instantly. I should have used it to bash in her skull.

"Alex isn't much," she cries at me. Now her eyes are narrow and full of sorrow, but she's a fraud and I know it. "He's pathetic. But he's mine. He does what he's told. He goddamn owes me."

I think back to what my father freak said before I obliterated him.

"I did what I had to do. I had no choice."

215

"You pulled the strings, Marie!" I scream at her. "You're the pathetic one!"

The knife sends a triangle of reflected light into my eyes and I blink.

"Guilt was Alex's motivator. Revenge on all the pretty girls was mine," she says, as she lunges with the blade pointed at me. "Now you've ruined everything."

In a flash, she's nearly on me and I do the only thing I can think of. I plant my foot between her legs and catch the base of the chair. It is fast and decisive. The knife falls to the floor. Marie Rader goes flying backward through the plate glass slider that leads to her patio.

Oddly, she doesn't scream.

She starts coming toward me again. I don't know exactly how I accomplish it, but I manage to plant my hands on her chair as she flails about. With all the strength that's somehow still inside of me, I push her through the glittery shards of glass on the patio toward her massive koi pond.

The one she bragged about while she was poisoning me with her ice tea.

The water surges over her head as she starts to sink down beneath the surface.

Instinctively, I return for the knife. I stand by the water's edge as Marie flails around. She's coughing and choking, but she grabs hold of the cement edge of the pond. I see her rise up. Those arms of hers. They are like a pair of pine trees. They undulate with muscle tissue. I see the veins in her forearms press upward like a mass of worms under her skin.

"Goddamn you!" she says. Her eyes are wild. She starts to

216

pull herself up and I do what I know I have to do.

And partly because I want to do it. I can't stop myself. I take the knife and slam its glinting edge through her fingers and she screams. Yet she hangs on. I stomp on her other hand with my shoes like I'm crushing the life out of a scorpion. Which she is, and at the same time, she's an insult to the creature. Her fingers are lying there on the edge of the cement and the water is turning to blood.

She goes under again.

The koi are drawn to her. I wish they were piranhas. I wish the waters were a vat of hydrochloric acid.

No matter. I am done. So is Marie.

Chapter Twenty-one

Cash: None.
Food: None.
Shelter: None.
Weapons: None.
Plan: Finish the job.

I KNOW I DON'T HAVE much time. Fuschia Lady told me she was watering her precious plants herself because she was leaving town and didn't trust the neighbor kid to do a thorough job. She's gone and she's the closest neighbor. That's in my favor right now. Marie and I made a lot of noise and I'm hoping no one else heard or cares enough to call the police. *The police*. Since Alex Rader was a cop, my respect for the cops has nose-dived. Rolland once said that the police are limited in what they can do, but I know that there was at least one among them—and maybe more—who do what they want no matter the price. Going to the police? Mom went there for help and look how it turned out for her. It is one thing of two that I know she and I will agree on. The other is that Hayden must never know what I know to be true. Like Mom, I carry that burden now. I love my little brother too much to have him live a life knowing that his heart circulates poisoned blood.

Like mine.

The koi pond is red with Marie's blood and I feel sorry that the fish have to swim in the filth of her body. Even so, I kick her fingers into the water with the tip of my shoe. Under the surface I see her face. Her eyes are open and so is her mouth, in a permanent scream. She was handicapped but she put up more of a fight than her husband, the worthless pig.

I start for the living room and though I scan it with speed I still see everything and capture it in my memory forever. Like a camera with my finger on the shutter. Click. Click. Click. The scene, the furnishings. Everything is mundane. A TV sits across from a sofa. A recliner points toward the set and a basket containing needlework sits at the end of the carpet ruts left by Marie's chair. I grab the wedding photo of Alex and Marie, smash the glass and pull the photo from the frame. Folded, it goes in my pocket.

The ruts. My eyes trace the worn parallel lines in the carpet throughout the house. They stop at the only place Marie cannot go.

The door that leads upstairs.

If Alex Rader had wanted to keep a souvenir from the prying eyes of his wife then it would be where she could not follow. He wouldn't have to lock it. I turn on the light and head up the steps. It is one large room with the dormers looking out toward the street. Alex Rader has set it up as his office. It is like no office I could have imagined. Yes, I've seen porn. Never on purpose. Not really. There have been times when

I've gone online and clicked the wrong link and in an instant I'm in a world of naked bodies moving and emoting in ways that indicate great pleasure but frequently make little sense.

One time I saw something so strange I still don't know what they were doing. Or how many were doing it.

And truthfully, I don't want to know.

The room is paneled with a dark oak wood. Using the seams in the paneling as a guide, Alex Rader has taped up photo after vile photo. These are scenes so sickening that I have to steady myself as I try to take them in without vomiting. I wouldn't mind vomiting right now. But I don't have the time. I move closer to a section of the wall that holds a familiar face.

Megan Moriarty does the splits in her cheerleading uniform from Kentridge High School. It is one of the images of her that I'd seen online.

Next is Shannon Blume's picture, the same pretty, but sad-eyed photo that had appeared in the newspaper—the one that her parents held in their arms as they called out to the world for help in finding their daughter.

Leanne is there too. But this photo is not familiar. It was candidly snapped when she was caught down by the marina, unaware.

She was being stalked.

Next, are photographs of Mom. I almost lose my breath as I have no choice but to look at them. *I'm* in some of these photos. One was taken last year at the Seattle Center when my family went there for a textile show Mom said she had to see. We were being watched. Hayden, Rolland and I are looking at something by the International Fountain, a big water feature that looks like a steam punk version of a sea urchin.

But not Mom.

She's looking *at* the camera. Right at it. Her eyes look scared, pleading.

I remember nothing about that day that suggests anything peculiar happened.

Alex Rader was there watching us.

I move closer. Underneath the photos taken before the various abductions are pictures of my father raping and torturing.

And making me.

It was possible that he'd set a timer to shoot these photos, of course, but something catches my eye in the one of him on top of Leanne, her cut-off shorts, pulled down to her ankles.

I hear a thumping sound, but I'm so mesmerized by what I see, I ignore it.

I look closer at the photo. A reflection. I see Marie holding a camera. It's clear as day, on the shard of a mirror that hangs over the bed in the underground prison.

What the?

I pull down the photos. I am a maniac right now. There are dozens, but I claw at each one, tearing some, but bringing others off in perfect condition. I couldn't stop myself if I wanted to. I wonder who the other girls are. I think there are at least four more that were added to his collection. All are like the original four—blonde, blue eyed, slender, pretty. His type.

I hear the thumping, louder this time, and I turn around.

Using her one good hand and the stump that I'd made for her with the kitchen knife, soaking wet Marie has heaved herself up the stairs. She slithered. She could barely speak, but she is as mad as hell and she won't be denied.

"To get out of here," Marie spits out, "you have to get by me."

She has the knife in her hand. I see by looking past her that she used it like a rock climber to hoist herself up the stairway. A trail of water and blood follows her like a dying snail. Except, she's no snail. Marie is fast. Faster than anyone could have imagined. I have only been upstairs a few minutes and she's managed to track me. She's pulled herself toward me. Her hair is wet and soaked with blood.

"Do you realize what you've done?" I ask, as though someone so vile could even fathom it. "Do you realize how many lives you ruined?"

"Try being in a wheelchair," she says. "See how that ruins your life."

"Am I supposed to feel sorry for you? Am I supposed to think that your playtime photo sessions were the result of some deep-seated anger you hold at the world because your spinal cord was cut? Get real, Marie."

"You're not getting out of here alive," she says. The blade has been dulled by its use as a stair climber, but it could still inflict fatal damage if I give her the chance. Which I won't.

I take the desk chair and I spin it hard and fast in her direction. I'm losing some of the photos, but I can pick those up. Marie lifts her torso from the floor with those powerful arms—arms that were mighty when she was a swimmer, when she could hold her breath for a long time. She balances herself with her stump and tries to lunge for me.

I throw my body on the chair and it smashes into her, sending her screaming backwards down the stairwell. When she lands, I see the tip of the knife. During her loud tumble, the blade finds its way behind her, entering her neck and protruding through her mouth as she falls back on it.

I can barely breathe. I stand there for a beat, watching as red oozes over Marie Rader's knife-tongue. Her light pink shirt is now a bloody red tie-dye.

I hear sirens and I know I have to get out of here right now. I gather up the photos and skirt past Marie's slumped body, her withered legs, her tree-trunk arms and that pie-cutting knife protruding from her gaping mouth.

By the door, I see my mom-style purse. I grab it, stuff the photos inside, run out of the door and through the hedge to the street. I know my fingerprints are all over the house, but I've never been arrested and there's no trace of me in anyone's system.

At least, not yet.

Chapter Twenty-two

Cash: $5.
Food: None.
Shelter: None again.
Weapons: Scissors, ice pick, Xanax, screwdriver.
Plan: No idea.

I CATCH MY BREATH. OR I try to. I take half a Xanax only because I have a bottle of them in my purse and I've been through a lot. A doctor would probably tell me it's OK and I almost laugh out loud at the thought. I don't need anyone's permission. Not after all I've been through. I've killed two people and while I'm a basket case, it isn't because of that. It's because sickness turns in my stomach when I think about the evil that had visited those families. How they suffered for years and years and had no one to help.

I walk from the Raders' street to the main road and plan to wave down the first car that I see. I try to make myself look normal by straightening up a little. I brush my hair, put on some lip-gloss, but there's no disguising that I look a little unhinged. I'm grateful that I'm wearing black jeans because I'm pretty certain that the wetness I feel on my legs is Marie's blood.

A car finally pulls up.

"Can you help me?" I ask when a woman rolls down her window.

"You want me to call someone for you?"

"Thank you. My phone's dead, my car just broke down back there and my sister Courtney is in the hospital. I was trying to get there. I don't know what's wrong with her."

"I'm so sorry," the woman says. "I'm going that way. I could drop you."

"No. No. That's too much to ask," I say, knowing that she's doing the same thing Leanne, Shannon, and Megan did. She's offering to help.

"No problem. Get in. My name's Shelly."

"Thank you," I say. "I'm Ginger."

The woman smiles. She looks to be about forty with a short bob and the kind of light touch with make-up that says she's a no-nonsense do-gooder. Just what I'm looking for right now.

"I haven't heard that name in a long time," she says. "Hop in."

I almost want to answer back that up until a few days ago, I had never heard that name before, except as an ingredient for holiday cookies.

"Family name," I offer, shrugging.

We chitchat for a few minutes. Her purse is next to me, a sight that makes me nearly smile. Five dollars isn't nearly enough for a night at the decidedly not-so-posh Best Western. While she drives I take her cellphone and some cash from her purse on the floor between us, then I crack the window because her car is clean and I know I can't smell that great. Shelly's words come at me, but only every other one truly registers. An ambulance races toward us and she pulls over.

Another follows.

I know where they are going, but I also know they will be too late.

She drops me at the hospital by the entrance to the ER. In the bright light there, I notice blood on my left arm and I wipe it on my pants. As the taillights of Shelly the Samaritan disappear I follow the road down the hill to the Denny's.

WITH HAIR THAT LOOKS LIKE mine, she sits at the counter. My mom. The one who isn't to blame for any of what happened to her.

But is to blame for all that she did to make it right.

As I approach, she looks down at a coffee cup and moves the spoon through the hot black liquid. I know she's only doing that because she's nervous. She doesn't use cream or sugar. I know everything about her.

Except everything I needed to know.

"I cleaned things up," I say, in a voice that is soft when it could so easily be sharp.

She spins around and her face is awash with joy. It is Christmas, New Year's, the Fourth of July, all rolled into one. I see how beautiful she is. I see how tortured she's been. She wraps her arms around me and I start to tremble in her arms. The waitress, counting her tips at the end of the counter, moves away. Mom hugs me hard. I could strangle her, but I don't. The reunion we're sharing means something to me after all. A truce. I don't cry. At least not in the way that most people do. I let the tears fall inside. She holds me like the warmth of a tropical ocean. I let her believe that I'm all right.

That she is forgiven.

"I got these for you," she says, indicating a paper bag with a shirt, pants and a jacket inside. I notice that she's wearing new clothes too. Or if not new, clean. A top and jeans that I've never seen before.

"Goodwill box around the corner. I was able to get inside," she says in a low, conspiratorial tone.

I hand her the purse.

"I got this for you. From the lost and found on the ferry to Seattle. We have a hundred and nine dollars. That'll get us a room for tonight."

I don't tell her how I got the money. She already knows what I am capable of doing when I am called to do it.

I get up and warn her not to look inside the purse.

I leave for the restroom and lock the door. This is the second time that I've used this restroom as a refuge. It should be my office. My stinky sanctuary. The mirror holds my image and I throw water on my face. I'm thinking. I'm wondering. I don't know if I should do it. I don't know what I could say to him that would make a difference. After all I've been through—all I've done—I don't have the guts to call him.

I chicken out and text him a message.

C—this is R. I'm staying at the Kent Best Western Motel with my mom. We're both OK. I will be gone tomorrow. I'd like to see you one last time. This is not my phone and I'm going to get rid of it now. I don't need a phone-tracking app to find me when

227

the police come looking for me. I'll be in the lobby at 5 a.m. If u
don't want to come, I understand.

And then I push SEND.

I smash the phone with my heel and toss it in the back of the toilet tank. Some more cool water on my face then I emerge wearing a clean sweater over a shirt and a pair of pants that are too short, but I roll up the hems.

"Thanks for the capris," I say.

Mom smiles. She's overdoing it, but I understand. She's always had a need to try to skew things toward normal.

"Something to eat?" she asks. "Cherry pie looks to die for."

I shake my head.

"No, thanks."

I will never even look at a cherry pie again.

Chapter Twenty-three

Cash: $12.
Food: Vending machine stuff.
Shelter: My favorite motel.
Weapons: Scissors, ice pick, screwdriver.
Plan: Say goodbye.

BEFORE WE GO TO BED, I go downstairs to the front desk, give back the screwdriver I stole, and purchase a large envelope with enough postage to send the photographs, including Marie and Alex's wedding pic. I address them to Monique Delmont because I don't trust the police and I know Leanne's mom will know what to do with it.

Inside, I enclose a handwritten note.

Dear Mrs. Delmont,

I hate to bring you so many terrible images of your daughter, Leanne. I am including them in this envelope, along with photographs of others and some documents, so that you might clear the names of the men who were smeared by the real killers, sheriff's detective Alex Rader and his wife Marie. Arnold Cantu did not murder Leanne. Kim Mock did not kill Megan Moriarty. Alex Rader's brother killed Kim. Michael Rader was the guard who supposedly found Kim's body in his prison cell. Steve Jones did not kill Shannon Blume. He's innocent and you need to help get him out of prison.

Alex and Marie Rader were sick, but smart. They picked girls from three different police jurisdictions. They planted evidence and faked police reports. You'll see some of that here.

Finally, more than anything, I want you to know that if not for your daughter's selfless act, my mother would not be alive today. Leanne was brave and kind.

Yours,

Tracy

I write another note, but I don't send it to anyone. Instead, I put that one in my pocket. When I return to the room on the second floor, I bring a can of Orange Crush from the vending machine next to the elevator. Mom immediately smiles when she sees the familiar packaging when I enter the room.

"You used to beg for that when you were little," she says from the bed.

I give her a knowing smile. "You used to tell me it was no good for me, but you let me have it anyway. Want some?"

The ice bucket is filled and waiting next to the sink in the little foyer outside of the bathroom. As Mom makes small talk from around the corner, I crush four Xanax caplets and dissolve them in one of the two drinks I prepare. *Her drink.* I know that the amount of medicine won't kill her. God knows I love her and want her safe, but I also know that the circumstances of my life and who I am don't allow for the comforting arms of a mother.

There are two beds in our room, but she calls me over to sleep next to her. We sit upright for a while as the TV plays on mute. She says how much she likes my new haircut. I tell her that she'll be amazed by what I did with Hayden's hair.

"I really love him," I say.

"I know," she answers, sipping more of the pop. The ice tinkles in her glass. I watch the level of the orange liquid drop lower and lower.

"I'll always think of Rolland as my real dad," I tell her.

This makes her sob a little, but I need her to know that. I need her to hear one more thing.

"I forgive you, Mom," I whisper.

She closes her eyes and I snuggle next to her. I am four. We are in Iowa. The trees that form a canopy over our backyard fill the sky. Fireflies move like micro bolts of electricity. I'm ten. We are in Minneapolis. Hayden is a toddler and I hold him while we watch TV on a snowy afternoon. I am fifteen and we are in Port Orchard in the kitchen she loved, chopping tomatoes and peppers for salsa. I laugh at something stupid she says and I watch her flip it right back at me.

All of those things and a million more flow right by like a speeding jet. I catch all that I can and then move to the next.

At 4:45 a.m., I slide away from Mom. She doesn't move, but I can feel her warm breath against my cheek when I kiss her.

The soundless television is sending a pale blue moonlight glow over her face. I will never know exactly what it is to be her, but she can never know what's inside of me either. I put the note on the nightstand next to her, along with the last $12 I have stolen from people who helped me, however unwittingly.

Dear Mom,

This is my turn to leave you a letter. Go to Ginger's and take care of Hayden. Enroll him in a real school. Give him a normal life. He deserves it too. So do you. I will always love you, but I need to do for others what can't be done by anyone but someone like me. Someday I might come back. I might not. I'm counting on you and Hayden to be, well, you and Hayden. Don't look for me. I know how to hide. My mother was a very good teacher.

All my love,

Your daughter

Chapter Twenty-four

Cash: None.
Food: None.
Shelter: None.
Weapons: None.
Plan: Tell him the truth.

THE AIR OUTSIDE OF THE Best Western is chilly, but I've been cold before. A lot colder. Try Nebraska in February. With every second after 5 a.m., I begin to accept that Caleb Hunter's not coming. I try hard to believe that he didn't get the message. *That's it.* That he would have come if he had. And yet I know if the roles were reversed, I wouldn't. I am used to being alone and slipping away without a goodbye. That's how I have been raised. I have never been more lonely in my entire life. I used to think that standing in the hallways at South Kitsap that the kids around me were parasites, evil beings that would try to harm me if I got too close. When the isolation came, it turned from a thin force field to an impenetrable barrier.

Until Caleb talked to me one day.

I practice what I want to say to him, though I know by

now he won't come. The words are scrambled like when my family made the switch and tossed all the potential boy and girl names in a plastic mixing bowl. I can still feel my fingertips pulling out the names that had been culled from all kinds of sources—magazines, newspapers, or a name we'd heard on the radio. How I prayed I wouldn't get it when Mom put in the name Stevie. I so didn't want that singer's name.

There's security in randomness.

The words that I put into the bowl of what I want to tell Caleb include goodbye, thanks, love, tears, fraud, forgiveness, and hope. I don't know the exact order, but as the time sweeps past the hour I'm more and more sure that I won't get to say them.

It is still dark and I start walking from the parking lot toward the street. It's slickened and shiny from rain. Spots of motor oil rise up and create opalescent paisley shapes on the surface of the blacktop.

My stepfather is dead.

Mom's drugged in a hotel room.

My biological father is dead.

My brother is with an aunt he doesn't know.

And, fittingly, I guess I'm alone.

And as I begin to feel sorry for myself—and with good reason, I think—I hear it. My heart rises inside my ribcage. I turn to look at the noise that I know can only be one thing. Caleb Hunter's white VW bug, the one that his mother had decorated with a daisy sticker that despite his best efforts left a residual adhesive that collected dust and dirt, making the daisy reappear. He hated that sticker. But he loved his mom.

He pulls alongside me and I stand there like a statue.

"What are you waiting for?" Caleb says, rolling down the window. He looks at me with those dark brown eyes and he flashes that smile that does what it always did. Disarms me. Leaves me wanting to be close to him. To hold him and let him know that outside of my family, he is the only one that I have ever loved.

"Rylee, or whatever the fuck your name is, get in!"

My feet start moving over the wet sidewalk. I grab the car door handle and slide into the passenger seat. In the backseat, I notice a backpack.

"What did you do to your hair?" he asks. "You look like shit."

Caleb never lied to me.

"Thanks," I say.

"Welcome."

He presses the gas pedal and the car moves onto the empty street toward Mount Rainier, a presence that dominates the landscape to such a degree that we northwesterners call it the Mountain. As if there could be no other.

Like the boy next to me. I know that as long as I live, there will be no other.

We drive mostly in silence to a park along the edge of the Green River and watch the sunrise through the foggy windshield. I tell him almost everything. I hold very little back. Not because I don't trust him, but because there's so much to say. While I face the blush colors behind the Mountain, he looks straight at me, unblinking.

"You're not a sociopath, are you?" he asks a little teasingly, trying to make the air in the VW a little bit lighter. "I mean, if you are, no offense."

I know by my broken heart that I am not. I'm something between normal and unfeeling. Unfeeling when I need to be. Normal when I let my guard down.

When I'm with him.

"No," I say, "I don't think so."

I make a note to myself that it probably would be a good idea to look up more about the clinical definition of antisocial personality.

Just in case.

He tells me everything he knows—and it's a lot. Apparently there is a law enforcement manhunt across Washington for me and Mom. I know the news cycle will change when Monique Delmont gets the package, but not the hunt for me. That will continue. He tells me that Gemma is going to be on national TV to talk about our friendship and has been buzzing about it at school for two days.

"Not Caradee?" I ask.

"No. Only Gemma. She supposedly was your BFF."

I don't mind and I say so. "Good for her. She always wanted to be on TV."

The sun is up now and we get out and walk along the river's edge. The gravel crunches under my feet and it reminds me of the quarry, but I don't bring it up. I've told him everything, but in broad brushstrokes. The phrase "gory details" comes to mind and I fully understand the meaning of it. I spare him most of the gory details.

His hand brushes mine as we sit on a bench and I die just a little inside.

He talks about his mother's death, his father's big insurance payoff and how his father's assistant from work moved in a few months after. Her name is Carmen and when he says it, he always hyphenates it with the word Bitch.

"I can't stand Carmen-Bitch," he says, a theme to which I'm familiar. "She's moved all my mom's stuff to the garage and, get this, told me that the reason she did it was because it was too painful for Dad. Like I don't matter and like he cared about Mom."

"I'm sorry," I say. I could probably do something about it, but not now.

He looks into my eyes.

"The world is an ugly place," he says. "You make it better."

If it were any other guy, I'd want to slap him for such a cheap line. But I know that there is such goodness inside Caleb Hunter that he truly means it.

"We belong together," he says, Taylor Swifting me, but I don't care.

I feel it too.

Since it seems as though he's never going to do it, I lean in and find Caleb's lips with my own. I'm Sweet Sixteen. I'm alive. And for the first time, I know what it feels like to choose a path of your own. The kiss is soft, sweet. It's watermelon in the summer. It's a field-picked strawberry in May. I want more, but I pull away. Now. There. This isn't the time or place.

I know for sure what has always been there from the first moment that we met.

Caleb and I do belong together.

Chapter Twenty-five

Cash: None.
Food: Whatever we need.
Shelter: VW bug (which I now call Daisy).
Weapons: None.
Plan: Vengeance.

AFTER THE KISS, CALEB LISTENS to my plan and I drift off to sleep as we drive east on Interstate 90 over the Cascades toward Spokane. We stop in Ellensburg and Caleb withdraws $400 from his father's bank account, the maximum allowed by his bank's ATM per day. He's a smart boy, but I could teach him a few things.

My first lesson will be at the Idaho Department of Motor Vehicles in Post Falls, Idaho. When we arrive at the DMV office there I ask him to pull into the back of the nondescript building where I get out of the car.

I walk toward the dumpster like I'm about to greet an old friend. In a way, I am. Mom and I survived one particularly lean spring on food we liberated from a dumpster. She would hoist me to the edge and I'd drop in like I was a paratrooper behind enemy lines.

Despite the grossness sometimes found there, I kind of loved doing it. It was a treasure hunt of necessity.

"We have money," Caleb calls out after me. "We don't need to do any dumpster diving."

"For what I need, we do," I say while he looks on, embarrassed that anyone will see me as I lift the lid of the big green receptacle and climb inside.

It takes me only a few moments to find what I need.

I emerge with a handful of driver's licenses. All had been rejected because the driver in question didn't like his or her photo. When I return to the car, I fan them out like a Las Vegas card dealer.

Caleb can hardly believe his eyes.

Yes, I have a lot to teach him.

"I'll use this one," I say, looking at a young woman with her eyes semi closed.

"You don't look anything like her," he says.

I close my eyes partially and hunch my shoulders a little.

"How's this?" I ask.

He laughs. We both do. The release feels good. Not as good as the kiss. But like a breeze, some of what I'd been holding inside passes through me. Gone.

Caleb looks at the license and makes a face. "Am I supposed to call you, what? Juanita now? Is that how this works?"

"No." I shake my head. "But that's a good question. I'll get back to you on that."

I sort through the rejects quickly. While most of the licenses belong to women who loathed their photos, there are a couple

239

of men and teen boy rejects that might work, even though they aren't nearly as handsome as Caleb Hunter.

But then, in my eyes, no one is.

"Take these," I say. "They'll come in handy someday."

He drives the car around the building and parks next to the spot where a trio of teens are waiting to take their exams. One is a girl. She's a redhead with pale white skin and freckles that remind me of Hayden's shoulders when he's been out in the sun. She looks nervous and I want to tell her that driving is not so hard. I've never had a real lesson and I do all right. I can't parallel park, I bet, but who really needs to ever do that in Idaho?

"Watch and learn," I say as he turns off the ignition.

Caleb follows me into the DMV. There is a line of people with bored-to-tears expressions all over their faces but I stomp my way to the front the second a patron steps away from the counter. I have two choices just then—a female or a male agent. Mom taught me to always go with the man if crying is a necessity.

This guy is in his forties, with gray-at-the-temple hair and wire-framed glasses that suggest neither hipster nor loser. He had a crisp blue shirt and is as neat as can be. The woman is wearing a sweatshirt with a horse on it.

He's a good choice, I think.

"I'm going to be in so much trouble," I say, tears already in place by the time I make it to his station.

He thinks I'm number 321, the color flashing on the screen for the next available DMV agent. Some big guy with a beard is, but seeing my tears, he backs off.

"How can I help you?" the DMV agent asks.

"I was in here earlier and some jerk put a big dent in my mom's car. Her brand new Nissan Juke! I'm going to get blamed for it. I tried to get his insurance information, but he wouldn't stop."

"I'm sorry about that, miss," he says.

I wrap my arms around myself like I'm trying to contain my concern when, in fact, I'm just warming up.

"What am I supposed to do?" I ask, managing a terrified look in my teary eyes. At least, that's what I'm going for. Terrified sometimes looks crazy. I dial it down a little. "My mom's got a mega temper." I let the tears flow down and a woman in a leopard top and black jeans approaches.

"Help her," she insists, taking off her sunglasses to ensure that her look is a searing one. "Can't you do something?"

"Please sit down," the agent tells her, looking at the slip of paper in the lady's hand. "342 won't be called for awhile."

"Government employee," she sneers. "Don't give a crap about the people."

"Hell yeah," says the big bearded guy, with lug-bolt-on-sidewalk voice.

The woman turns to me and pats me gently on my shoulder. "I am a witness. I saw what he did. We should call the news."

I wouldn't have picked that leopard top if my life depended on it, but I like her. A lot.

After consoling me and making the DMV agent feel about two inches tall, she takes her seat along with the others, now all riveted by what's going on at the counter.

He looks at me, then the crowd. He's befuddled.

"What can I do about it?" he finally asks.

I don't wipe my tears. The more evidence of my distress, the better.

"I have his license number," I say. "Maybe that'll help?"

He shakes his head. "I can't look it up. That's against policy."

I cry some more, this time a whole lot louder.

"My mom's going to kill me. It's not my fault."

The woman is back, and with her, the bearded guy. They are now a team. That's nice.

"Help her," she says with a glare of disdain in her eyes, aimed like a rifle at the clerk. "Do something right for a change. Just because you hate your job doesn't mean you have to hate the world."

"What this lady here just said," the bearded guy snaps.

The DMV man looks around. I see sweat blooming from under his arms. As disgusting as that is, it looks like a pretty good sign to me. Plus the fact that I'm pretty sure the beard guy drives a Harley.

"Let me see your ID?" he asks, as though he needs to follow some rule when breaking another one.

I slide the license from the dumpster over to him.

He looks at it, then at me. My heart beats a little faster. There's always a slight risk in this part but I know that he won't help me if he thinks I'm from out of state—and if that's the case, why am I at the DMV in the first place? I'm there, of course, because it isn't the police station, and outside of that, I figure only the DMV would have access to the confidential information that I need.

"Juanita," he finally says, "you can't say you got this

242

information from me. I could lose my job."

I sniff a little, but not too much.

"I won't, sir," I say. I give him the license number of the van from the truck stop. He provides a name and an address in St. Maries, Idaho. He hands me a pen and some paper to write it down, but I don't need to. I'll remember it just fine.

I turn around and the crowd is with me.

"Thank you," I say loud enough for everyone to hear. "Our government really does care about us."

It was a lie, but the guy in the sweaty blue shirt deserves some kind of praise.

I play that address over in my head.

I know the little girl is not named Selma, but in my mind I still call her that. From the business center at the Best Western, I printed out an article about her from the internet. I know her name is Angie Starr and that she'd last been seen in a park in Missoula, Montana. Her hair is different in the photograph to what it had been through the window of the van that early morning when I saw her draw that sad face, but I know how easy it is to change a girl's appearance.

I've done it all my life.

Caleb, who is nearly speechless by my performance, and I walk out into the bright light of the parking lot with a new sense of purpose.

I know that I will find the girl.

I will find *him*.

Kill him.

My name is Alexandra. I was named for my biological father, a serial killer who tortured and murdered at least three teenagers and raped my mother sixteen years ago. He's dead now. I know for a fact that I'm stronger than he ever thought I could be. The people who understand where I come from are the people who matter.

The ones Caleb and I can help.

Don't miss HUNT, the next Vengeance novel
from Gregg Olsen – coming soon . . .

Q & A with Gregg Olsen

You have written both fiction and non-fiction, including True Crime. When writing RUN, did you feel that the knowledge you have of real-life crime helped or hindered your plotting?

Definitely helps. Over my years I've had the privilege (and I do consider it so) to tell the true stories of people who have survived the unthinkable. That fuels all of my fiction. *RUN* was no exception. There's always a nugget of truth in all of my fiction. Early in my career, I wrote about a woman who'd been poisoned and family members were all but certain that her husband – the stepfather to a fifteen-year-old girl – was guilty. Ultimately, he was proven not to be the killer, but as I wrote *RUN* I thought of that girl and all of the emotions she had that came with thinking that someone close to you was a killer. Of course, *RUN* is complete fiction, but the heart of any good story is the conflict and emotion that comes with the action. The plotting is organic, just like real life. I let my characters take me where they need to go. Sometimes, I'm not the boss. ☺

When writing crime fiction, inevitably you will lose characters you grow attached to. Do you feel an emotional attachment to any of the characters in RUN?

Yes. Rylee. I love her tortured spirit and her ability to be clever, kind, and yes, ruthless. For the right reasons, I think. As I wrote the book I was rooting for her all the way. She seemed more real to me than any character I've ever created. I like her and I want her to find happiness and strength in life in a very real way. I know where she wants to go . . . and I want to help her get there.

Rylee has to make some tough decisions on her journey to find her mother's captor, including leaving her brother behind. Will we see more of Hayden in the next book?

I'm plotting *HUNT* right now and I will have some Hayden in it. As tough as Rylee is, she's come to know different kinds of love. She knows that her brother and her connection to him is a mixed blessing for sure. She protects him in real ways, but most importantly in making sure her mother doesn't tell him the truth.

Rylee's discovery of who her real father is fills her with rage, and it is this anger that gives her the courage to track down her mom's captor. Is there power in rage, or is it purely dangerous?

That's a tricky question. Personally, I believe strong emotions, passions, are good if channeled in the right way. Who wants to live his or her life feeling nothing? Isn't it better to take that emotional energy into something positive?

If you were going on the run and could only take one thing with you, what would that be?

A book. Kidding. An untraceable credit card. A sack of money. Actually, if I was on the run I'd take my dog Suri. She's a mini dachshund – so she's completely portable. She's great company. And she is as fierce as they come. I wouldn't need a knife, a gun, or any kind of weapon. Suri would take on even the most formidable foes. Maybe even a serial killer.

What inspires you to write?

My readers do. It's really that simple. I write to reach people. There can be no other reason.

Do you have any tips for budding writers?

My advice is always the same. If you think you are a writer, then you are. To be a *good* writer you need to practice. When I say practice, I mean EVERY DAY. I tell new writers that whatever project they are working on must be tended to daily. Even if only a few lines. A paragraph. Whatever. Writing can be difficult and almost all writers look for ways to get out of doing the hard work of the job. If you make it a routine, a promise, a commitment, you'll have something. I promise. I'm not saying it will be easy, but nothing worth doing really is.

Gregg Olsen

A *New York Times* and *USA Today* bestselling author, Gregg has written nine non-fiction books, nine novels, a novella, and contributed a short story to a collection edited by Lee Child. He is one of only a few authors to have appeared on both the fiction and non-fiction *New York Times* bestseller lists.

In addition to US and international television and radio appearances, he has been featured in *Redbook*, *USA Today*, *Wall Street Journal*, *People*, *Salon*, *Seattle Times*, *Los Angeles Times* and the *New York Post*. His young adult novel, ENVY, was the official selection of Washington State for the National Book Festival.

A Seattle native, Gregg lives in Olalla, Washington with his wife, twin daughters, three chickens, Milo (an obedience school-dropout cocker spaniel) and Suri (a miniature dachshund so spoiled she wears a sweater).

Follow Gregg at:
www.greggolsen.com
Twitter: @Gregg_Olsen
Instagram: greggolsen

ALSO FROM

HOT
KEY
BOOKS

Lona Sixteen Always has lived nearly all her life as someone else. She spends twenty-three hours a day on the virtual reality 'Path', reliving the memories of a boy who lived twenty-five years ago. Then one day a long-lost face appears on Lona's screen, and she is wrenched brutally into a life that is suddenly all her own. But Lona discovers there is a heavy price to pay for straying from her chosen path …

IN FIVE DAYS SHE WILL COME

SAY HER NAME

JAMES DAWSON

Bobbie Rowe is not the kind of person who believes in ghosts. A Halloween dare at her boarding school is no big deal, especially when her best friend Naya and cute local boy Caine agree to join in too. They are ordered to summon the legendary ghost of 'Bloody Mary': say her name five times in front of a candlelit mirror, and she shall appear ... But, surprise surprise, nothing happens. Or does it?

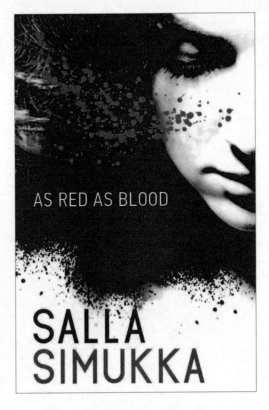

AS RED AS BLOOD

SALLA SIMUKKA

Coming soon:
The first part of a thrilling new
Nordic crime series

Lumikki Andersson is hardly your average teenager. She lives alone in the city of Tampere, Finland, and has a firm rule to mind nobody's business but her own. But she finds herself caught in an increasingly tangled web of deception, corruption and danger, and navigating Tampere's dark underbelly in the search to expose its shocking connection to the international drugs trade. Lumikki is smart, but is she smarter than a master criminal? Can she bring down the infamous 'Polar Bear' – or will she become another one of his victims?

Read on for an extract from Salla Simukka's
AS RED AS BLOOD – coming soon …

All around lay glittering white. Over the old snow, a new, clean layer of soft flakes had fallen fifteen minutes earlier. Fifteen minutes earlier everything had still been possible. The world had looked beautiful, the future flickering somewhere in the distance ahead, brighter, more peaceful, more free. That was worth betting everything on one last card. Trying to make a clean break was a terrible risk but the only way forward.

Fifteen minutes earlier a light, downy snowfall had spread a thin feather blanket over the old snow. Then it had ceased, as suddenly as it had begun, followed by rays of sunshine breaking through the clouds. Hardly any days all winter had been this beautiful.

Now each moment saw more red intermingling with the white, spreading, gaining ground, creeping forward along the crystals, staining them as it went. Some of the red had flown further, a shrieking bright crimson spattering the snow.

Natalia Smirnova stared with brown eyes at the red-flecked snow, seeing nothing. Thinking nothing. Hoping nothing. Fearing nothing.

Ten minutes earlier Natalia had hoped and feared more than ever before in her life. With trembling hands she had stuffed banknotes into her genuine Louis Vuitton handbag, all the while listening for even the tiniest rustling from outside. She had tried to steady her nerves, assuring herself that everything was fine. She had a plan. But at the same time she had known that no plan was ever perfect. An intricate edifice carefully constructed over months can collapse at the barest nudge.

The handbag had also contained a passport and plane ticket to Moscow. She wasn't taking anything else. At Moscow airport, her brother would be waiting with a rental car, ready to drive her hundreds of kilometres to a *dacha* only a few people knew about. There her mother would be waiting with three-year-old Olga, the daughter she hadn't seen in more than a year. Would her little girl even remember her? But no matter. A month or two hiding out in the countryside would give them time to get to know each other again. While they waited until she believed they were safe. While they waited until the world forgot about Natalia Smirnova.

Natalia had stifled the nagging voice in her head that insisted no one would forget her at all. That they would not allow her to disappear. She had assured herself that she was not so important that they couldn't simply replace her when the need arose. And going to the effort of tracking her down would be too much bother anyway.

In this line of work, people disappeared now and then. Usually taking some money along with them. That was just one of the risks of doing business, an unavoidable loss like the spoiled fruit a supermarket had to toss out.

Natalia hadn't counted the money. She simply stuffed as much of it as she could in her bag. Some of the bills had crumpled, but that didn't matter. A crumpled five-hundred-euro note was worth just as much as an unwrinkled one. You could still buy three months' of food with it, maybe four if you were really careful. You could still use it to buy one person's silence for long enough. For many people, five hundred euros was the price of a secret.

Natalia Smirnova, age twenty, lay face down, her cheek in the cold snow. Not feeling the prickling of the ice against her skin. Not feeling the frigid chill of twenty-five degrees below on her bare earlobes.

The land is strange, and cold is its spring

Natalia, you are freezing

The man had sung that to her in a gruff voice, off-key. Natalia hadn't liked the song. The Natalia in it was from Ukraine, but she was from Russia. She had liked the man singing and stroking her hair though. She had just tried not to listen to the words. Fortunately that had been easy. She had known some Finnish, understanding much more than she could speak herself, but when she stopped struggling and let her mind relax, the foreign words ran together, losing their meaning and becoming nothing more than combinations of sounds falling out of the man's mouth as he hummed against Natalia's neck.

Five minutes earlier Natalia had been thinking about that man and his slightly clumsy hands. Would he miss her? Maybe a bit. Maybe just a little bit. But not enough, because he had never loved her, not really. If he had loved her, really loved her, he would have solved Natalia's problems for her, as he had promised so many times. Now Natalia had to solve her problems for herself.

Two minutes earlier Natalia had snapped shut her handbag,

bulging with cash. Quickly she had tidied up and then glanced at herself in the front hall mirror. Bleached blonde hair, brown eyes, thin eyebrows, and shining red lips. She had been pale, with dark circles under her eyes from staying up too late. She had just been leaving. In her mouth she had tasted freedom and fear, both of which had a metallic tang.

Two minutes earlier she had looked her reflection in the eyes and raised her chin. This was her opportunity to make a break, and she was taking it.

Natalia had heard the key turning in the lock. She had frozen in place, straining her ears. One set of footsteps, then another and a third. The Troika. The Troika were coming through the door.

All she could do was run.

One minute earlier Natalia had charged through the kitchen towards the terrace door. She had fumbled with the lock. Her hands had been shaking so much she couldn't get the door unlatched. Then, by some miracle, it had opened, and Natalia had run across the snow-covered terrace into the garden. Her leather boots had sunk in the snowdrifts, but she had pressed on without looking back. She had not heard anything. She had thought for a moment that she might make it after all, that she might escape, that she might actually win.

Thirty seconds earlier a pistol fitted with a silencer had fired a dull snap and a bullet had pierced the back of Natalia Smirnova's coat and skin, barely missing her spine and ripping through her internal organs and finally the handle of her Louis Vuitton bag, which she had been clutching to her chest. She had fallen forward into the pure, untouched snow.

Now the red puddle under Natalia continued to spread, consuming the snow all around. The red was still voracious and warm but cooled as each second passed. One set of slow, heavy footfalls approached Natalia Smirnova lying in the snow. But she did not hear.

Thank you for choosing a Hot Key book.

If you want to know more about our authors
and what we publish, you can find us online.

You can start at our website

www.hotkeybooks.com

And you can also find us on:

We hope to see you soon!